D1547114

# The Realest Killaz

Tranay Adams

**Lock Down Publications and Ca$h
Presents**
# The Realest Killaz
**A Novel by *Tranay Adams***

**Lock Down Publications**
P.O. Box 944
Stockbridge, Ga 30281

Copyright 2020 by Tranay Adams
The Realest Killaz

First Edition August 2020
Printed in the United States of America

**Lock Down Publications**
**Like our page on Facebook: Lock Down Publications**
**@**
www.facebook.com/lockdownpublications.ldp
Cover design and layout by: **Dynasty Cover Me**
Book interior design by: **Shawn Walker**
Edited by: **Nuel Uyi**

# Stay Connected with Us!

Text **LOCKDOWN** to 22828 to stay up-to-date with new releases, sneak peaks, contests and more…

Thank you!

## Submission Guideline.

Submit the first three chapters of your completed manuscript to ldpsubmissions@gmail.com, subject line: Your book's title. The manuscript must be in a .doc file and sent as an attachment. Document should be in Times New Roman, double spaced and in size 12 font. Also, provide your synopsis and full contact information. If sending multiple submissions, they must each be in a separate email.

Have a story but no way to send it electronically? You can still submit to LDP/Ca$h Presents. Send in the first three chapters, written or typed, of your completed manuscript to:

LDP: Submissions Dept
P.O. Box 944
Stockbridge, Ga 30281

*DO NOT send original manuscript. Must be a duplicate.*

Provide your synopsis and a cover letter containing your full contact information.

Thanks for considering LDP and Ca$h Presents.

Tranay Adams

# Chapter 1

## 1993
## *Mexico*

Joaquin was born into some very unfortunate circumstances. His mother, an Afro-Mexican woman named Marcella, was a whore working inside of brothels in Tijuana. One night, a sexual encounter with one of her frequent jawns resulted in a broken condom and Joaquin growing inside of her. Unfortunately, Marcella didn't want children. In fact, she hated them. She looked at her being pregnant as a hindrance to her making pesos. She knew her pimp would allow her to be with child and still work, but she didn't know if all of her jawns would be comfortable with getting sexed by a pregnant woman. With that in mind, once her pregnancy started showing, Marcella started dressing in baggie clothing. Later, she'd find out that the tricks she fucked with didn't mind sexing a pregnant woman. As a matter of fact, they all enjoyed it. It was something about her pregnancy making her pussy warmer and wetter.

Marcella ended up making a lot more money while she was pregnant than she did when she wasn't. The men with whom she turned tricks paid big for her services, and they tipped even bigger. Eventually, the day came for Marcella to give birth to her baby boy. She went through labor alone inside a trashy alley crawling with roaches and rats. When she finally managed to pull baby Joaquin out of her pussy, he was covered in slime and blood, crying aloud. The raggedy toddler mattress Marcella had given birth on was soiled with blood, piss and shit. She had cleansed her bowels while attempting to push out her infant son. About thirty minutes later, Marcella squirted blood from her womb, and the rest of the placenta—which was attached to baby Joaquin's umbilical cord—came out. She gnawed on the umbilical cord until it was severed from the baby, cleaned herself with sanitary wipes from her purse, and placed the baby inside a trash bin.

"Es un mundo frío y cruel, pequeño. Sugiero que crezcas para ser exactamente igual (*It's a cold and cruel world out there, little one. I suggest you grow to be exactly like it*)." Marcella pulled her hair back into a ponytail and tangled a rubber band around it. She kissed her fingertips and touched them to baby Joaquin's lips. She removed the gold beaded rosary from around her neck, and looped it around the infant's. Her face wrinkled with disgust, seeing a golden German shepherd munching on her bloody placenta. Shortly, a stray cat wandered over and started licking her blood up from the toddler mattress. Reaching inside her purse, she pulled out a pack of smokes and placed one of the cigarettes between her lips. After sparking it up, Marcella blew out a cloud of smoke and headed back to the brothel to see if she could find herself another jawn. There was money to be made!

Baby Joaquin cried and cried until he eventually drew the attention of the German shepherd, the cat and six rats, which crawled around the edge of the trash bin he was inside of. A woman dressed in niqab—and pushing a baby stroller—stopped in front of the alley. Her personal body guard, a Mexican man with hair like John Wick's, draped in an expensive dark purple suit, stopped beside her. Their faces frowned as they listened closely to the crying baby. They exchanged glances, realizing they'd heard the child somewhere inside the alley. The bodyguard pulled out his gun and motioned for the lady in the niqab garb to follow him. He went down the alleyway cautiously. He had to move carefully because, for all he knew, he could have been walking his charge into a trap. He'd been hired to protect Griselda Torres, the Mexican woman in the niqab attire, with his life. Being the wife of Mateo Torres, the boss of Blood Brothers Inc. Cartel, she most definitely was targeted by rival cartels, mainly The Brown Hands of Death Cartel. The main reason Griselda wore the niqab was to conceal her identity from her husband's enemies.

"The baby is in the trash bin!" Griselda scowled, and pointed at the dog and cat. "Get rid of the animals, Nolan!"

Nolan, the bodyguard, pointed his gun up into the air and squeezed the trigger twice. The resonating gunshots scared off the dog and the cat, sending them hurrying down the alley. Using his gun, he knocked the rats off the edge of the trash bin and tossed the empty boxes aside. Hearing the baby Joaquin's crying growing louder and louder, Nolan continued to toss aside the empty boxes and newspapers until he found him. He tucked his gun back into its holster and scooped baby Joaquin out of the trash bin. He hadn't been holding him a minute when Griselda approached and extended her arms for him. Nolan passed baby Joaquin to Griselda, and she bounced him gently in her arms and hushed him.

"It's cold out here, I know. You're hungry too. That's why you're smacking your lips and moving your hands to your mouth, huh? I've got you. Momma's gonna take good care of you." Griselda removed her niqab and wrapped baby Joaquin in it, snuggly. Nolan looked around to make sure no one was around to see her face. There wasn't, but he knew it was best she still kept her identity secret. He took out his sunglasses and slid them onto her face. Then, he pulled out his handkerchief and tied it around her nose and mouth.

Nolan frowned upon seeing Griselda pulling one of her breasts out of her bra. "What're you doing, Mrs. Torres?"

"What's it look like? I'm gonna feed 'em. There's no telling how long he's been out here. His lil' self must be starving." Griselda placed her nipple inside baby Joaquin's mouth, and he instantly stopped crying. He sucked milk from her tit and shut his eyelids, balling up his little fists. He was definitely hungry. "See? That's all he needed." Griselda smiled from behind the handkerchief. Hearing her baby boy crying in the stroller, she looked over her shoulder at him. "You're hungry too, huh, Ignacio?" Griselda looked to Nolan. "Nolan, give Ignacio his baby bottle while I push his stroller, please."

"Yes, ma'am," Nolan replied, doing like she'd asked. As soon as Ignacio got the baby bottle, he quieted down.

Griselda cradled baby Joaquin in one arm while she pulled Ignacio in the stroller. Nolan led the way, keeping a close eye on their surroundings, and his hand near his gun. He stepped outside of the alley, looking up and down the block, making sure the coast was clear. Once he saw there wasn't a threat in sight, Nolan motioned the chauffeur in the bullet-proof Mercedes-Benz truck over. The Mercedes SUV sped over quickly. After making sure Griselda and the babies were secured inside the truck, Nolan hopped into the front passenger seat and slammed the door shut. He signaled to the chauffeur to drive off, and contacted Mateo through his ear-bud, letting him know they were on their way back to his villa.

\*\*\*

Initially, Mateo didn't want anything to do with a child that wasn't his, when Griselda brought baby Joaquin home.

Over time, he grew to love him like he loved his own son—Ignacio—and treated him as such. Some would argue that Mateo showed favoritism between the boys, but that wasn't exactly true. Joaquin got just a little more attention than Ignacio from his parents because he was an orphan, and they felt like they had to make up for it. Ignacio became jealous of Joaquin and despised him. The boys got into more fist fights than they could count on their fingers and toes. Once, Ignacio had literally tried to kill Joaquin. He would have succeeded too, if it wasn't for Mateo interfering and then taking a switch to Ignacio's ass.

Joaquin had gotten tired of the drama between him and Ignacio, and tried to make amends. He wanted to get along with Ignacio so that they all could be one big happy family. He loved Mateo and Griselda as much as he loved Ignacio. It didn't make any sense for them to be at each other's throat. He knew that if he or Ignacio ended up seriously hurting or killing the other, the Torres would be devastated. And that was the last thing that he wanted.

Although Mateo loved and cherished Joaquin like he was kin to him, he wasn't of his bloodline. Ignacio was. So it was only right that, when the time came, he'd sit at the head of the table of his organization. While Mateo went on to school Ignacio on how to run his business, he sent Joaquin out into the trenches to train under his chief enforcer, Madrid. He wanted him to become a stalwart soldier in his cartel, so he sent word to his top dog to treat Joaquin like he'd treat the rest of the recruits. There wasn't to be any favoritism when it came to Joaquin. He made sure Joaquin understood such as well.

Mateo saw the future when it came to his empire. He saw his successor, Ignacio, at the helm of his operation once he'd passed away, while Joaquin and the rest of his soldiers would back him with the muscle. Mateo was too busy focusing on all of the pros the union between his sons would bring. But then again, he forgot to add up the pros and cons.

\*\*\*

## 2005

Joaquin's eyelids narrowed into slits as the hot sun shone on his face. Toying with the gold beaded rosary hanging around his neck, he took in the appearance of the recruits on either side of him. Most of them looked like they were his age, or older. The balding chubby Mexican man beside him looked to be about thirty-five, or forty years old. He was easily the oldest of them present. There were twenty of them in total. Besides, they all had one thing in common—they were all dirt poor and doing everything they could to make ends meet. Hell, that's the exact reason why they were there—money.

The cartel soldiers that recruited the men promised them a small fortune, but they were full of shit. Cartel hit-men really didn't get paid much. They made about as much as a factory worker, which was about $105 a week in Mexico. However, they did get five to twenty thousand dollars for a hit and whatever drugs they wanted. This was to their boss's own benefit, though. The cartel hit-men had to be under the influence to carry out some of the horrific acts that they did. On top of that, with a lifestyle that involved fighting with the police and rival cartels, hit-men had a very low life expectancy. It was like they were working for a temporary employment agency. You'd be here today and gone tomorrow.

Hearing the sound of a huge vehicle approaching, Joaquin looked down the road. He saw a big yellow school bus coming in his direction. The bus pulled to a stop before him and the rest of the recruits. He looked at the windows of the bus, and saw his reflection staring back at him. Joaquin was a handsome youth of an almond skin tone His light-brown eyes took on the color of honey when confronted by the sun's rays. He had long curly hair that spilled down to his shoulders. He usually kept it in an untamed afro, but today he was wearing it in two braids on either side of his head. His attire was a T-shirt, blue jeans, and Chuck Taylor Converses.

Joaquin looked to the doors of the bus as the rotund driver activated them, making them open. Right then, a forty-five-year-old Mexican man made his way down the short black steps and onto the ground, chewing tobacco. A scar lay over his right eyebrow and over his cheek. A second scar traveled from the side of his head, and over the other scar on his cheek. He rocked a shaved head and a salt-and-pepper goatee. His attire was a navy blue T-shirt, which he wore under a military tactical, bullet-proof vest with several pockets on it. He had on camouflage pants and black combat boots. A machete was sheathed on his left side and a handgun was holstered on his right. He had an M-16 assault rifle hoisted over his shoulder. This man was known as Madrid, Mateo's chief enforcer and leader of his hit-squad. His soulless eyes and menacing aura made his presence known wherever he was. He'd been bodying shit since he was nine years old. Killing was an art to him, and he looked at himself as Picasso.

Silence fell on Joaquin and the rest of the recruits as soon as Madrid's booted feet touched the ground. They all stood upright, chest out, chins up, with their hands at their sides, like army cadets standing in line. Madrid spat a loogie on the ground, and wiped his mouth with his gloved fist. He strolled down the row of men standing before him, taking each and every one of them in from head to toe. Each of the young men present was handpicked by the boss, Mateo. Madrid was familiar with all of them, especially Joaquin.

"Alright, for those of you who don't know me, I'm Madrid," Madrid told them as he paced the ground before them. The nigga had that M-16 out in the open for everyone to see like it was legal. It was like he didn't give a shit about the police seeing him with it, and he didn't. Mateo had the law dogs in his pocket, so he was good. "I'm gonna be your instructor for the next three months. If you can hack it, I promise you'll be the meanest, gun-toting, killing machines that have ever walked God's green earth." He turned around and began to stroll back down his row of potential killaz again. "Make no mistake, ladies—we're in the business of killing. Now, if you think you don't have the stomach for it, I suggest you grab your shit and beat your feet on down the road. Because once you're on that bus, your brown asses belong to me until your dick's put in the dirt. Do we have an understanding?"

He stopped and turned around to his men. They nodded their understanding. "Good. Now, grab your shit and get your asses on the bus!" The young men grabbed their backpack of belongings, and made their way toward the bus. They weren't moving fast enough, so Madrid took the M-16 from off his shoulder, cocked it, and pointed it into the air. He pulled the trigger, and the assault rifle bucked in his hands, spitting fire. Empty shell casing leaped out of the M-16 and hit the ground, smoking. The loud noise from the automatic weapon made the young men pick up the pace. They ran toward the bus and up the steps, finding their seats on it. Once Madrid's cadets were loaded on the bus, he spat on the ground again and made his way upon the vehicle, cradling his M-16. The bus driver closed the double doors behind him, shifted gears and drove off, leaving a cloud of dirt behind them.

Joaquin stared out of the window as the bus made its way around the mountain. He was nervous. His hands were clammy. He didn't know what challenges lay ahead for him, but he knew without a doubt that he was going to conquer them all. He had to. He needed to prove to Mateo and the others that he was cut out for this shit. Mateo, Griselda, and Ignacio were the only family he had. And he feared if he didn't meet the expectations of Mateo, he'd be exiled like Moses. The thought of that terrified him. He already stuck out like a sore thumb in Mexico. He was one of the few black faces there. He felt like an alien in a strange world, and all he had were The Torres. If he was to lose them now, he'd be devastated and lost. And he'd be damned if he allowed that to happen.

"Alright, our stop is coming up," Madrid said, which drew Joaquin and the rest of the recruits' attention. When they turned their heads, they found him standing in the aisle, slinging the strap of his M-16 over his shoulder. "Gentlemen, I'd like to welcome you to your home for the next three months." Right when he said this, the passengers stood up and looked out of the windows, drinking in their surroundings. Coming upon the mountain top, they found several dead bushes that were partially green and the color of hay. There were also an old, raggedy navy blue Toyota pick-up truck with four big lights mounted on its rooftop, and two vans. About six cartel henchmen stood out in the open. They were all strapped up with AK-47s. They wore either bandanas around their necks, or ski masks rolled up on their heads like beanies. Strapped against their bodies were either tactical vests that resembled the one Madrid was wearing, or black or white Kevlar bullet-proof vests. The henchmen were laughing and talking. They were also smoking cigarettes and taking swigs of Coronas.

"Okay, y'all sit tight," Madrid told the recruits. The bus driver had told him in Spanish to tell the young men to sit down because he was about to make a wide turn. The cadets followed Madrid's orders while Madrid held on to one of the seats, trying desperately to keep his balance during the wide turn of the bus. Once the bus driver completed the turn, he pulled up about twenty feet away from where the pick-up truck and the vans were parked. He then killed the engine. Afterward, the bus driver flipped down the sun-visor to block out the sun, cracked open a tall can of beer, and picked up a nude magazine dedicated to Latinas. He busied himself flipping through the pages and taking the occasional sip of his beer.

"I want chu guys to grab your shit and follow me off the bus in a single file." Madrid took the time to take in every face accounted for. "Okay, let's roll out." He motioned for them to follow him out of the bus. The recruits grabbed their things, and followed behind him out of the bus. Madrid stopped his stroll once he neared the other cartel hit-men. He exchanged some words with them in Spanish. The killaz put out their cigarettes and either tossed their 40 ounce bottles of beer aside, finished drinking them, or screwed the caps on them, and sat them down by their boots. They then put on their game faces. They looked intimidating with their balled up faces of anger. They were all straight-up killaz, certified head busters, with at least one hundred bodies apiece under their belts. They were trained to go and kill without a conscience—on Mateo's orders.

"Grab the body outta the back of the pick-up and drop 'em over here!" Madrid told two of the cartel hit-men in Spanish. The men adjusted the straps of their assault rifles on their shoulders and jogged over to the flatbed of the Toyota. They opened the flatbed and grabbed a dead body, which was under a bloodstained white sheet. One of them grabbed the legs of the body while the other grabbed it under its arms. Together, they carried it over to Madrid and laid it down before him. As they stood upright, one of them grasped the sheet and yanked it free from the lifeless, naked body. The body that was underneath the sheet was of a forty-five-year-old Mexican man with long hair and a thick beard. Both the hair on his head and the hair on his face were covered with a sprinkling of gray. The man had craters on both of his cheeks. There was a black gaping hole in the center of his forehead, where a single bullet had entered. The middle-aged man had been dead for quite some time, so his complexion was powder blue and his lips were purple.

Madrid unsheathed his machete and flipped it over in his palm. The blazing sun kissed off the shiny metal blade and cast a rainbow. Madrid took a look over the faces of the recruits. He lifted his machete and played "eenie meenie miney mo" with them until his machete landed on the Mexican teenager at the center of the cadets present.

"You, Juan, get cho tall, skinny-ass over here!" Madrid motioned him over with the machete. It was ninety-degrees outside, so it was hot as fuck. All of the recruits were sweating, especially Juan. Sweat oozed out of his pores, and slid down the side of his face. He looked mad nervous and afraid. He didn't know what Madrid required of him. But he hoped that he didn't want him to dismember that dead body, because he was sure he couldn't stomach it.

"You—you want me?" Juan asked him with raised eyebrows and a finger pointed at his chest. He was a lanky kid with fluffy, bouncy black hair reaching the end of his neck. He had a mole above his top lip and a few hairs that had sprouted out of his chin. He was dressed in a brown T-shirt which was torn around the collar, and blue jeans that were torn at the knees.

"Pendejo, you're the only fucking Juan here, now get your brown ass over here! Now!" A scowling Madrid barked at him. Juan dropped his things at his raggedy sneakers, and took off running in Madrid's direction. Madrid shoved the machete into his arms, smacked him upside the head, and gave him a swift kick in the ass. The kick sent him spilling to the ground, and dropping the machete. Juan scrambled over to the machete and grabbed it. Madrid ordered him over toward the dead body, and he hastily crawled over to it. He looked up at the chief enforcer as if to say, *Now, what do I do?*

"I want you to chop off one of his arms," Madrid pointed to each body part, calling them out in Spanish. Juan looked up at Madrid with pleading eyes. The teenager looked hesitant to follow Madrid's orders. Madrid looked away from Juan and pulled his nose, taking a frustrated deep breath. He turned his frowning face back toward Juan and drew his gun from its holster, pointing it right between his eyes. Juan's eyes doubled in size, and his mouth flung open. He dropped his machete and threw his trembling hands into the air. He went to plead for his life, but it was already too late. Madrid pulled the trigger of his gun. A bullet ripped right between Juan's eyes and sent blood and gray brain matter flying out the back of his skull. Juan fell to the ground, and sent a dirt cloud into the air. He lay there staring out of vacant eyes, his mouth wide open. Madrid injected his smoking gun back inside his holster. He looked over the recruits and saw horror etched across their faces, as they stared down at a dead Juan. They couldn't believe that Madrid had blown the young man's head off in front of them. They knew shit was damn real now.

"You see 'em?" Madrid asked as he pointed his gun at Juan. "Hesitation and cowardice will not be tolerated within this organization. The jefe wants soldiers. Soldiers that'll follow orders—no questions asked!" He took a moment's pause, before pointing his gun at Joaquin. "You, negrito, chop off his arm. Now!" Madrid's mouth shot off like a starter pistol in a race. Joaquin, realizing that his life depended on a fast reaction, hurriedly snatched up the machete. He got down on his knees and outstretched the naked dead man's arm. He focused his eyes on the dead man's arm and lifted the machete above his head. Joaquin's pupils looked up at Madrid, who was watching him with a serious expression across his face. The heartless killa had his hand resting on his holstered gun. There wasn't any doubt in Joaquin's mind he'd be next to die if he didn't follow his command. With that in mind, Joaquin diverted his eyes back to the dead man's arm and brought the machete down with all of his might. Blood splattered against Joaquin's shirt and face. Joaquin's mouth swelled up as he was about to puke. He put the back of his bloody hand against his lips, and looked up at Madrid. He made an ugly face, as he swallowed the vile lunch he'd just brought up through his esophagus. He wanted to vomit, but feared Madrid would kill him if he did.

Joaquin looked back down at the chop he'd delivered to the dead man's arm, and found his hand was halfway attached. So he lifted the machete above his head again and brought it down. The machete went right through the wrist bone, severing it completely from the dead man's arm. He then held it up for Madrid to see. Madrid took his hand off of his holstered handgun and motioned Joaquin over to him. Joaquin got upon his feet and walked over to Madrid, handing him the severed hand, which dripped blood onto the dirt. A wicked smile spread across Madrid lips, which revealed the gold fangs inside of his grill. He slid his wet tongue across his top row of teeth. The gold fangs twinkled.

"Good job, negrito, very good job." Madrid ruffled Joaquin's hair in a playful manner. Joaquin fixed his hair as best as he could, wearing a confused expression on his face, not expecting Madrid's reaction. Madrid held up the severed hand and showed it to everyone. The cartel henchmen applauded and whistled cheerfully. The rest of the cadets slowly began to clap, as if they weren't sure if it was safe to do so or not. "Guess I've got myself a new back-scratcher, huh?" Madrid stuck the dead hand under his tactical vest and scratched his back with it. All of the cartel killaz laughed their asses off. He then tossed the dead man's hand aside, and told Joaquin to get back in line.

"Okay, you," he pointed another one of the recruits with the machete, which he'd taken from Joaquin. A chubby man with a balding scalp came running forward. Madrid passed him the bloodstained machete and told him to chop off the dead man's other hand.

The chubby man got down on his knees, held down the dead man's wrist and raised the machete high above his head. Grunting, he swung the machete downward with all of his might. *Chomp!* Dots of blood clung to the chubby man's face.

The recruits learned that the only way to escape from the camp was through death. In three months they'd learned how to handle every gun from a .44 magnum revolver to an AK-

47. They were taught how to handle knives and machetes. They also learned how to ambush their enemies, and how to kill, among other useful skills pertaining to their trade. The camp was like an ISIS-style school, where men with a fascination for the criminal lifestyle were trained to be bloodthirsty killaz. The training turned the recruits into psychopaths, purging them of fear and empathy. They were able to kill without mercy or remorse. They spent most of their time hunting and killing the soldiers of rival cartels, cutting up bodies and torturing other members of their own organization that didn't follow orders.

\*\*\*

## 2010

It was seventy-six degrees with the occasional breeze; the perfect weather for people to be out soaking up the sun, or swimming in a pool. If it hadn't been for his current situation, that's exactly what he would've been doing. But instead, he was down on his knees with his wrists zip-tied behind his back, at the edge of a deep ditch, five of his comrades to the right of him. His face was beaded with sweat, and he could smell the foul stench of piss and shit. Some of his comrades had defecated on themselves with the thought of death lingering over their heads. From the corner of his eye, he could see some of them trembling with fear. He couldn't believe it. Together, they had given men, women, and even children the same fate that awaited them, but here some of them were—petrified of dying. All he could do was, shake his head in pity for them. He would go out like a man when it was his time. He knew what he was getting into when he signed up to be a soldier in the Brown Hands of

Death Cartel. He knew that death and/or imprisonment came with the territory, and he made peace with that a long time ago. In his lifestyle you never knew when your number was going to be called, but you knew death was inevitable. Like the saying goes, 'If you live by the gun, then you die by the gun'. Still, even when you knew you were living on borrowed time, it was kind of hard to prepare yourself for the end of your life.

When he'd gotten up that morning, showered, brushed his teeth, combed his hair and had gotten dressed, he didn't know the last thing that would go through his mind would be a hollow-tip bullet.

*Blam!*

Broken skull and bloody pieces of gray brain matter went flying everywhere when a bullet smashed into the back of his head. He fell forward, and his lifeless body went tumbling down in the ditch. Blood poured out from the back of his head, as the look of death shone on his face.

Scowling, Joaquin lowered his chrome, long-barreled .357 magnum revolver with the black rubber grip. He was wearing a red bandana over the lower half of his face. Joaquin had grown into a handsome young man. His only flaw was the quarter-inch scar that lay over his eyebrow and eyelid. He wore his long, naturally curly hair in eight neat cornrows, which had a couple of hairs out of place. His attire was a white T-shirt, over which he wore his tactical bullet-proof vest. Tan cargo pants and black combat boots completed his ensemble.

At just seventeen years old, Joaquin had over one hundred bodies under his belt. That's not including the poor soul he'd just slumped over into the ditch. Ever since he had devoted his life to Mateo's cartel, he had become desensitized to violence. He looked at it as a necessary evil.

When he was sent on a mission, there wasn't a soul that was spared—besides children. He didn't believe in murdering innocent kids. That wasn't in his bag, but he'd allow the men in his company to do so. Although killing a child wasn't a part of his modus operandi, it didn't stop him from earning his bones as one of the coldest killaz in the drug game. He was well-known among his peers and their bosses as well. Hell, some of the bosses of rival cartels had even tried to recruit him, but his loyalty belonged to his father's organization. And there wasn't any amount of money or number of women he'd betray his family for. He wasn't like other men. He was cut from a different cloth. As a matter of fact, they didn't even make the fabric he was cut from any more.

*Blam!*

*Blam!*

*Blam!*

Joaquin went down the row of men and blew their brains out, one by one. With each shot he delivered, the bound man would slump over and tumble down into the ditch. When the time came for the fifth man to be put out of his misery, he sprung to his feet and took off running. The soldiers, a part of the cartel that Joaquin was working for, upped their machine guns to lay him down, but he lifted a hand to halt them. They obliged him and lowered their weapons. Joaquin took his sweet time, licking his thumb and sliding it across the sighting at the end of his barrel. The beaming sun caused the saliva on the sighting to shine like a small diamond. Joaquin squeezed his left eyelid shut. His nose scrunched up as he took aim, lining his barrel up with his fleeing victim's skull. Gently, he placed his finger on the trigger, waiting for the perfect moment, and then—he pulled it. The gunshot echoed, and the revolver recoiled as it released a single bullet, which rocketed out of the barrel, zeroing in on the escapee's skull. The man's head exploded like a rotten tomato, and he flopped to the ground, legs going up in the air.

Joaquin lowered his revolver as wisps of smoke came from its barrel. He looked off into the distance at the man he'd just gunned down. Seeing that he wasn't moving, he holstered his handgun and drew his machete. A bright gleam swept up the full length of the blade and settled at its tip, twinkling. Joaquin started walking toward a young Mexican man in a wrinkled white suit and sky blue button-down shirt with dirt stains on them. The Mexican man's name was Eduardo Maldonado. He was the pudgy son of Rubin Maldonado: the boss of a rival organization, *Las Manos Marrones De La Muerte*—The Brown Hands of Death Cartel. Eduardo was sobbing aloud, and yellowish green snot was hanging out of his nose. He was so terrified that he was shaking like a stripper at King of Diamonds. He was one of the men that had shit in his pants and pissed on himself. Joaquin shook his head shamefully, seeing how the heir to Rubin's throne was reacting to the early grave that awaited him. He couldn't believe Eduardo was the kind of man that Rubin's bloodline produced.

Joaquin grabbed a fistful of Eduardo's hair and yanked his head back, causing him to howl in pain. Eduardo continued to sob, and more snot oozed out of his nose, hanging from his chin like a thin rope.

"Por favor, por favor, no me mates, hombre! (*Please, please, don't kill me, man!*)" Eduardo cried aloud and pissed his pants again. The soldiers of the cartel laughed their asses off, seeing a grown-ass man reduced to a fucking baby. They got a real kick out of it.

"Deja de quejarte como una puta puta, Eduardo! Sé un hombre, amapola! Se un jodido hombre! (*Stop whining like a fucking bitch, Eduardo! Be a man, poppy! Be a fucking man!).*" Joaquin's face balled up angrily behind his bandana, and he gripped Eduardo's hair tighter, making him wince. "Look into the cell phone, mano, look!" He pointed to the soldier filming everything with his iPhone. Eduardo looked into the lens of the cellular as best as he could, with his head being held back. Seeing he'd complied, Joaquin went on to speak to his father, who the footage would eventually be sent to. "Esto es que pasa cuando follas con Blood Brothers Inc. Cartel (*This is what happens when you fuck with Blood Brothers Inc. Cartel!*)"

Joaquin cocked the machete back and swung it with all of his might into Eduardo's neck. The blade went halfway through his meaty neck, and blood gushed and poured out of it. Eduardo's eyes exploded open in agony, and his mouth flung open. His eyes rolled to their whites, making him look like he was possessed, and his bottom lip trembled. He took his last breath. So he didn't even feel the next three strokes of the machete, which severed his head completely from his body. Joaquin kicked Eduardo's headless body into the ditch, and it went tumbling down. He then held up Eduardo's severed head as spinal fluid and blood slid down his arm. He threw his head back and yelled, "The day belongs to Blood Brothers Inc!" The Blood Brothers Inc. Cartel soldiers standing behind him fired their machine guns into the air, as they repeated his words.

Joaquin rolled Eduardo's severed head toward his comrades and watched them play soccer with it. One of the soldiers acted as a goalie and stood in front of the ditch full of dead bodies, trying to block his comrade from scoring, but he managed to kick Eduardo's severed head past him. The head ricocheted off the dirt wall of the ditch and landed inside of it, upon another lifeless body.

"Bien, estaremos ahí! (*Okay, we'll be right there!*)," a familiar voice came from over Joaquin's shoulder. When he turned around, he found Madrid behind him, taking his finger away from the ear-bud in his ear.

Madrid looked exactly the same, except his head was shaven and showed signs of graying along with the goatee he'd grown. He'd taken a liking to Joaquin and molded him into his image. The most ruthless soldier of The Blood Brothers Inc. Cartel had grown to look upon Joaquin as a nephew.

"What's up?" Joaquin threw his head back, wondering what was going on.

"We've found Rubin," Madrid said. He then looked over his shoulder at the rest of their comrades, and told them the good news. Some of them started piling up into their pick-ups and jeeps, while the others shoveled dirt onto the corpses in the ditch.

"Good. Let's go get that son of a bitch!" Joaquin wiped him machete on his cargo pants and sheathed it on his hip. He then adjusted the strap of his machine gun on his shoulder, and began moving toward the dull red Toyota pick-up with the paint peeling on it. He'd taken two steps before Madrid placed his hand on his shoulder, stopping him. Joaquin looked at him with a furrowed brow, wondering why he was holding him up.

"Hold up, Joaquin, your father wants you back at his place," Madrid told him.

"What? What is it about? We've got business to attend to," Joaquin said.

"I don't know what he wants, but Ignacio told me that he wants you home pronto. So you get your black ass there,

ASAP." Madrid gave him a stern look, letting him know he meant what he said. Normally, Joaquin would have a problem with another man coming at him like the old killa had, but he had a tremendous amount of respect for him. "Take the motorcycle." Madrid pointed his thumb over his shoulder at an old motorcycle. It was comprised of different parts of older bikes, but it ran as good as new. Joaquin took a deep breath, and took the strap of his machine gun from around his neck, passing it to Madrid. He didn't want to draw attention to himself by riding around with the machine gun in the open. Madrid switched hands with the machine gun and pulled him close. He held him against him for a minute, before kissing him on the side of the head. He then looked him over, patted his shoulder, and headed towards the Toyota pick-up that was awaiting him.

Joaquin hopped onto his motorcycle, kicked the kick-stand up, cranked it up, and twisted its handlebars back and forth. The motor of the bike revved up higher and higher, and then he sped off, leaving a big dirt cloud in his wake.

***

The loose hairs of Joaquin's cornrows ruffled as he sped down the road on his motorcycle. He dipped between vehicles in traffic and whipped past people on the sidewalks. He bent a few corners and hit a few dirt roads before he was finally pulling up to the gates of Mateo's villa. Hands clutching the handlebars, Joaquin stood upright with his booted feet planted firmly on the ground, to steady his motorcycle. Soldiers stood on either side of the gate, holding M-16 assault rifles. Familiar with whom Joaquin was, one of them unlocked the gate and pushed it open. Once the path was clear, Joaquin rode his bike inside and killed his engine at the bottom of the steps of Mateo's house.

Joaquin made his way up the short flight of steps and rapped on the front door. He waited for a moment, but no one answered. His face frowned up. He wondered what was going on. He twisted the door handle and pushed his way inside, crossing the threshold. He closed the door behind him and made his way through the enormous house, looking around. Acknowledging that it was eerily quiet, he called out for his parents as he walked along, but he didn't receive any response.

"Oh, my god, Ignacio, what have you done?" Mateo's voice rang out from the dining room.

Joaquin looked alarmed when he heard his father's panic-stricken voice. Instantly, he took off running toward the dining room and pulling out his .357 magnum revolver. He slowed down as he entered the double glass doors of the dining room, which had sheer white curtains covering them. He twisted the door handle and pushed his way inside the dining room. He was just in time to see Ignacio gunning down his own father, Mateo. A horrified expression spread across Mateo's face, and he went sailing backwards in his chair, pulling the white flower printed table cloth along with him. He crashed to the floor, bringing a dark green bottle of red wine—and a glass of wine—along with him. The glass exploded upon impacting the surface, and left red wine everywhere.

Ignacio approached his father, clutching a silenced Beretta in his black, leather-gloved hand. The five-foot-seven pretty Mexican boy was wearing a navy blue turtle neck and a brown suit. His grayish blue eyes, accompanied by his slicked back hair and five o'clock shadow, made him look like an Italian fashion model.

"Son—Son—W—Why? I—I love you—" Mateo said weakly, outstretching his shaky hand towards Ignacio. The hole in his chest quickly expanded with blood.

"You never loved me, old man." Ignacio mad-dogged his father as he stood over him. "I'll tell you who you love. You love that mothafucking mayate, Joaquin. All you and mommy ever do is, brag about him and tell me how I should be more like him. I get tired of hearing that shit! It makes me wanna rip my fucking ears off!"

"I—I love you and—and your—your brother—equally," Mateo told him, as he continued to reach out to him.

"That mothafucking spade ain't my brother! Mommy shoulda left his black ass in the dumpster where she found him!" Ignacio spat angrily, seeing Mateo lying helpless on the floor. He spat a gooey yellowish glob on his father's face and kicked his hand away. He then blew a hole through his forehead, killing him instantly. Blood quickly poured out of the back of his head and pooled on the floor.

"Noooooo!" Joaquin screamed with tears in his eyes and pointed his .357 magnum revolver at Ignacio. He kept his gun trained on him as he took a moment to wipe the tears spilling down his cheeks.

"It's about time you showed up. Now the entire family is here." As soon as Ignacio said this, a pained moan came from the other side of the dining room. Joaquin looked to find his mother, Griselda, lying on her stomach and bleeding out of her mouth. She was wearing a salmon-colored dress with bees and flowers on it. She had two exit wounds in her back, from being shot, and the blood was quickly expanding. Her sun hat lay beside her.

"Momma!" Joaquin called out, and a fresh set of tears pooled in his eyes, sliding down his cheeks. He watched as her head dropped to the floor, and she took her last breath.

Her eyes were vacant, and her mouth was hanging wide open.

"This is your fault. You know that, don't chu?" Ignacio asked him. Joaquin looked at him like he was crazy, so he proceeded to let him know exactly what he meant. "You just had to weasel your way into my family and steal all of the goddamn attention and love my parents had for me. It isn't my fault that your mother left you in a dumpster! Why the fuck should I have to sacrifice what was rightfully my birthright just so you could feel wanted, huh?"

He waited for Joaquin to answer him, but he didn't. So he continued on with what he had to say. "Well, I'm taking over poppy's empire now! I'll be the one true boss of Blood Brothers Inc. Cartel. And you? Well, you get to join the family you always wanted!" Ignacio pulled out a .38 special from the small of his back and pointed it at Joaquin, pulling its trigger. A bullet ripped through Joaquin's arm, and he howled in pain as he collapsed. Ignacio tucked his .38 special into the front of his pants. He whipped out his handkerchief and bit down on it. Next, he squeezed his eyelids shut and pressed the Beretta into the flesh of his arm. As soon as he pulled the trigger, he screamed into the handkerchief and blood ran down his arm.

"Grrrrrr, son of a bitch!" Ignacio said. He then snatched the handkerchief out of his mouth and looked at his wound. It was bad, but he wouldn't bleed to death. He tossed the Beretta near Joaquin's still body and contacted the soldiers posted outside the gates of his father's estate through his Bluetooth earpiece. "Joaquin lost his mind! Mothafucka killed my parents and shot me! But I managed to take him," he turned around, but Joaquin had vanished from where he'd fallen, "—out!" *What the fuck?* Ignacio muttered under his breath. His eyes scanned the dining room, but he couldn't locate Joaquin anywhere. "He's gone! He's fucking gone! He's somewhere in the house! I'm gonna go after him! You guys get inside now! Now goddamn it! Now!" He disconnected the call and pulled out the .38 special from his waistline. Holding his injured arm at his side, he moved through the house with his revolver, leading the way. Hearing a door slam upstairs, he hurriedly ran toward the staircase and darted upstairs. He crept down the hallway, following the trail of blood.

\*\*\*

Joaquin ran inside his bedroom, slamming and locking the door behind him. He tied his red bandana around his shoulder to slow his bleeding, grabbed his knapsack from out of the closet, and ran over to the mini refrigerator. Hurriedly, he stuffed bottled water and sandwiches inside the bag. He loaded all of the documentation for his identification inside his sack. His identification card, social security card, passport, birth certificate, etc.

*Boom, boom, boom!*

The rattling of his bedroom door made him move quicker. He stuffed clothes, socks and underwear into the knapsack. He slung the strap of his knapsack over his shoulder and flipped over the mattress, revealing a chrome handgun with a black handle. He tucked the gun at the small of his back, and picked up the two fully loaded magazines beside it, stuffing them into his pocket. Joaquin made a run for his closet, but suddenly stopped in his tracks. He snapped his fingers as he remembered something. Darting back over to his dresser drawer, he grabbed three grenades and stuck them inside of his knapsack.

"Blow this bitch open!"

Joaquin's head whipped to his bedroom door, hearing Ignacio's angered voice from the other side. The next thing he heard was the sound of automatic gunfire shredding the door into splinters. A moment later, the lock of the door dropped to the floor. *Boom!* One of the two soldiers guarding the gates of Mateo's villa kicked the door open. He, the other soldier and Ignacio rushed into Joaquin's bedroom, guns up, ready to fire. Their necks were on swivels as they scanned the room thoroughly. Joaquin wasn't anywhere in sight, but his closet's door was wide open and its light was on. Instantly, Ignacio knew what was up. Joaquin's slick ass had gone through the duel entrance that was located inside of the closet. On the opposite side of the wall was his parents' master bedroom. The moment that thought entered Ignacio's head, he heard a loud crash coming from the opposite side of the wall.

"Come on!" With his .38 revolver, Ignacio motioned for the soldiers to follow him, and ran toward the closet.

\*\*\*

Joaquin came through the duel entrance and entered his parents' bedroom, slamming the closet door behind him. He then pushed the dresser in front of the door and kicked it over, barricading the closet's door. Next, he pushed the canopy bed aside and revealed a trap door. The trap door was the entrance of a tunnel that led to American soil. Mateo had the tunnel dug in case his enemies discovered where he lived and decided to launch an attack. He and his family would be able to flee their home and seek asylum in the United States. He'd always talked about taking up residence in Los Angeles, California, where all of the Hollywood movie stars and big time directors were. He always wanted to try his hand at show business. He wanted to write and direct movies. And he planned on using a portion of the money he made from drugs to bankroll his first film.

Joaquin pulled open the trap door by its handle, and found a ladder that led down straight into the darkness. He narrowed his eyelids, trying to see through the dark, but he couldn't manage to see jack shit. The banging against the closet door drew his attention. He knew time wasn't on his side, so he had to act fast. Joaquin made his way down the ladder as fast as he could. He'd gotten halfway down when he heard automatic gunfire again, and the soldiers kicking in the closet door.

He looked below, but he still couldn't see anything.

"Fuck it!" Joaquin said as he made up his mind to jump down into the unknown. Taking a deep breath, he leaped down to the ground and winded up falling awkwardly. It took him a minute to gather his wits, having knocked the wind out of himself. He fished around inside his pocket for his Zippo lighter. Pulling it out, he struck a blue flame with it, and it illuminated his face. "Oh, shit!" He ducked and dodged two bats as they flew past either side of him.

"Aye, he's down here!"

Joaquin heard one of the soldiers alert Ignacio and the others to his presence. He looked to see the soldier standing up right and pointing his M-16 down at him. He pulled its trigger and spat rapid flames at him. Joaquin jumped back, listening to the bullets ping and ting off the metal ladder, causing sparks to fly. Still holding the flame of his lighter, Joaquin searched the wall for the panel that activated the lights of the tunnel. As soon as he found it, he smiled and opened it. Looking down the tunnel, he flipped up the switches of the panel, and the bulbs lining the tunnel flickered twice before staying lit. Joaquin saw an old military jeep parked in front of him. He also saw rats scurrying the ground, and bats flying around.

"America, here I come," Joaquin said to no one in particular as he stuck his lighter back inside his pocket. He then grabbed one of the grenades out of his knapsack and looked to the ladder. The soldiers and Ignacio were coming down fast. He knew he had to get the fuck out of there. He didn't stand a chance in a shoot-out with them.

Joaquin tossed his knapsack into the back of the jeep and jumped into the driver's seat. The key was already inside the ignition. Simultaneously, he turned the key while mashing on the gas-pedal. The engine struggled to turn over, so he kept on trying it.

"Come on, baby! Come on!" Joaquin gritted and continued to try. He glanced in his side view mirror, and saw Ignacio and the soldiers coming his way, chopping at him. He ducked down to avoid the bullets, some of which slammed into the back of the jeep. Glancing in the side view mirror, he saw them closing the distance between them, still firing. The side view mirror got blown off. This really startled him, with the bullet coming so close. "Come on, sweetheart, daddy needs you, baby. Start for me, momma! Start for me!" Joaquin kept trying the ignition and the gas-pedal again, and the jeep roared to life. He floored the gas-pedal, and the Jeep sped off, with bullets pinging off of it. Joaquin glanced up in the rearview mirror, and saw Ignacio and them still on his ass.

*Unh huh, I gotta trick for y'all asses,* Joaquin thought, as he grabbed the grenade from the passenger seat, where he'd placed it. He pulled the ring out of it with his teeth, and spat it out of the vehicle. He clutched the grenade for a couple of seconds and then he threw that bitch behind him. It tumbled towards Ignacio and the soldiers, and stopped. One of the soldiers pointed at the grenade and shouted a warning to Ignacio and them in Spanish. They all took off, running in the direction they'd come from, but they didn't get far before the grenade exploded. All of their asses hollered as the explosion sent them flying in different directions, rocking the foundation of the tunnel.

Joaquin glanced in the rearview mirror for any signs of life, but he didn't see anyone moving around. He figured they were all blown to hell, and this brought a broad smile to his face. It took Joaquin a total of three days to make it to Los Angeles. Along the way he made pit stops to eat, drink and use the bathroom. He made sure to ration his food since he didn't have that much. On top of that, he didn't have much money to his name, so he had to be careful of how much he spent.

The military Jeep had run out of gas by the time he reached his destination. Once he came from underground, he had to hitch-hike his way through the streets of East Los Angeles. He stayed in tents on skid row, and slept at shelters when they weren't full to capacity. He made his living collecting recyclables and doing odd jobs. Once he'd gotten sick and tired of being down on his luck, he started robbing and stealing. Eventually he linked up with some Mexican gangbangers and started hitting licks with them. They wanted him to join their organization, but he decided to stay neutral. Shortly, Joaquin started doing the same shit he was doing in Mexico to stay paid. He was taking hits on niggaz for a profit. Any contract could get fulfilled. He didn't give a fuck if it was a cop that you wanted knocked off. As long as you could meet his price, then he was going to take the hit.

Tranay Adams

# Chapter 2

## 2005

### *Los Angeles*

Kershawn Hoyle was a six-foot-one caramel- complexioned man with freckles on his face and hazel green eyes. He wore his auburn hair in a tapered fade and a neatly trimmed goatee. He stood in front of the mirror of his nightstand, admiring his incredible physique, which was toned with muscle and pronounced with snaky veins. Kershawn was in impeccably great shape. He stayed away from fatty foods and decreased his sugar consumption. He drank plenty of water and worked out vigorously. The only thing he consumed that was unhealthy was homemade cigarettes. There wasn't anything he loved to do more in his spare time than read, indulge in a fine bottle of red wine, and burn down a stick of tobacco.

Kershawn slipped on his wife beater and tucked it into his jeans, fastening his belt. He placed his white Kevlar bullet-proof vest on over his head and strapped it to his body. Once he secured his Heckler & Koch P30 inside the holster at the small of his back, he strapped the ankle holster on and secured his black .32 automatic in it. Afterwards, he slipped a black T-shirt on over his head with *Bouncer* emblazoned across the front, together with a hefty black jacket and a black beanie that also had *Bouncer* on it. He pulled on a pair of black leather gloves, and concealed his black ski mask inside his jacket. On his way out the door, he snatched his keys off the dresser and turned off the light on his way out.

Kershawn made his way down the hallway, and stopped at his thirteen-year-old niece's bedroom. He rapped on the door for a while, but he didn't receive any response; so he pushed his way inside. The light shone on Billie's bed from inside the hallway, and he found her asleep, with her head under the covers. Thinking about his niece, a smile spread across Kershawn's lips. He'd never wanted kids of his own, so he wasn't exactly jumping for joy when he had to take custody of Billie. She winded up growing on him though, and now he couldn't imagine his life without her. He loved her like he loved the very air he breathed.

Kershawn looked at the nightstand, where there was a portrait of a six-year-old Billie. She was wearing a bicycle helmet, knee pads and elbow pads while sitting on a Barbie bicycle. Although Billie was missing four teeth from the top row in her mouth, she was wearing the biggest, cutest smile across her face. Billie was a cute caramel-complexioned girl with curly auburn hair, freckles and hazel green eyes. She bore a striking resemblance to her uncle Kershawn, but that was probably due to the fact that she was the daughter of his identical twin brother—Dershawn. Unfortunately, Dershawn and his girlfriend, Theresa—Billie's mother—were murdered. Ever since then, which was four years ago, Kershawn has had full custody of Billie. He was a strict guardian. He had her cooking, cleaning, doing homework, and being home from school at what he thought was a decent hour.

Still smiling, Kershawn walked out of Billie's bedroom, pulling the door shut behind him. He then walked inside the kitchen, through the door of his garage, and hopped into his whip. Once he fired it up, he activated the garage door opener, and drove out into the night's cool air. Unbeknownst to him, Billie was hiding inside the trunk of his car. She believed her uncle was a bouncer at some gentlemen's club called The Pussy Kat Club until a week ago. He didn't know it, but she spied on him when he'd come home later than usual one night. She'd noticed the dry blood splattered on his shoes and lips, as well as the bullet-proof vest strapped to him. She saw him pick the mashed slugs from off it and discard them. On top of that, he'd disappeared throughout the day for hours, with an explanation of his whereabouts that didn't make sense. If that wasn't strange enough, he had two cellular phones. One of which was a prepaid cell phone that he always left the room to talk on whenever she was around.

Billie didn't know exactly what her uncle did for a living, but she was sure he wasn't a bouncer at a goddamn strip club. She believed he was into the street life, but she didn't know what aspect of it exactly. One thing was for sure though: she was going to find out this night.

\*\*\*

Kershawn pulled his whip a few houses down from the house where his mark lived. After he killed the engine, he grabbed his black ski mask from out of the glove-box, and a folded up document. He looked the document over; it was paperwork for a divorce. Folding it back up, he slid it back inside of his jacket and pulled his ski mask down over his face. He looked into the rearview mirror and adjusted the mask, so he could see out of it. Afterwards, he took his gun from underneath the seat, cocked it and hopped out of his car. Slamming the driver's door shut, he threw his hood over his head and took in his surroundings. There wasn't anyone out on the block, and—except for the crickets in the grass—there wasn't any noise.

Kershawn stuck his hands inside his jacket's pockets and walked upon the curb. He made his way down the sidewalk, oblivious to the fact that he'd brought his niece along on his mission. It took Billie some time, but she finally managed to push the back seat down. She crawled out and eased her head upward, watching Kershawn to see what house he was going to go in. Seeing him enter the yard of a big white house, with a picket fence, she eased out of his car and quietly shut the door. She pulled the hood of her sweatshirt over her head, and sped-walked down the sidewalk. She kept a close eye on things as she moved. Realizing it was best she kept up with Kershawn, Billie broke down the block in a full sprint. By the time she reached the white house, her face was shiny from sweat. Huffing and puffing, she wiped her sweaty face with her hand and watched her uncle attentively.

He was on the porch, kneeling before the front door as he tried to unlock it with the assistance of his credit card. He'd occasionally glance over his shoulder to make sure he wasn't being watched. Once Kershawn had popped the lock, he slipped his credit card into his back pocket. Next, he slipped on a pair of brass knuckles over his fists. After making sure the lethal weapons were secure on his hands, Kershawn twisted the doorknob gently, and slowly pushed his way inside the house.

As soon as Kershawn disappeared inside his mark's crib, Billie hopped the fence with one hand and darted alongside the house. She made it to the kitchen window, where she found an older white man standing at the microwave. He was whistling as he drummed his fingers on the roof of the microwave, waiting for his TV dinner to finish heating up. The white man was of average height, with thinning hair and a protruding belly. He was dressed in a button-down, with his sleeves rolled up, a tie, and slacks. As his food was warming up, he removed his glasses and fogged its lenses with his hot breath. He then whipped out a handkerchief from his back pocket and wiped his glasses clean.

Having stopped, the microwave started beeping; so the man slipped his glasses back on. Opening the microwave door, he touched the TV dinner a few times to test its hotness. Making note that it was safe to grab, he removed it from the microwave and peeled off the transparent covering. He balled it up and shot it over into the trash can. He hummed as he opened the silverware drawer, and removed a fork and knife. Bumping the drawer closed with his hip, he made his way back over to his TV dinner. He prepared to cut himself a slice of meatloaf, when he thought he heard something inside the living room. His forehead creased, and he poked his head in the doorway, but he didn't see anyone. Figuring it was a figment of his imagination, he shrugged and started back over to his dinner. He ate a slice of the meatloaf and smiled with his eyelids closed, chewing. He savored the flavor of the juicy slice of meat.

Unbeknownst to the man, Kershawn was leaning up against the wall beside the kitchen doorway, waiting for him to make his exit. The man grabbed a bottle of Budweiser out of the refrigerator, popped its cap, and took a swig of it. He then tucked a napkin into the collar of his shirt, picked up his TV dinner and started for the doorway. He was still whistling on his way out of the doorway. He'd just taken his first step across the threshold, when his eyes bulged as a masked Kershawn jumped into his path. Swiftly, Kershawn gave him a punch to the gut, knocking the wind out of him, and making him drop his meal. He followed up with a left-right combination to his face, and finished him with a kick to his chest. The impact from the blow sent the white man hurling backwards inside the kitchen. Dizzy, he slammed up against the stove and landed on his ass. He saw double, watching Kershawn pick up the beer bottle he'd dropped when he assaulted him. He shook off his dizzy spell, and with a growl, he charged at his assailant. Kershawn sidestepped him and swung the bottle at the back of his head. The bottle exploded on impact, sending broken glass and suds of beer everywhere. The white man collided with the floor, grimacing.

"I see you gotta lil' fight in you, Jeremy, well, that's good, 'cause I could use the cardio," Kershawn told the white man, watching him struggle to get upon his feet. He waited until he was on all fours before he cocked back his leg, and kicked him in the stomach. The swift blow flipped him over onto his back, and left him lying flat out, wincing. He then started stomping and kicking him. Once he'd gotten tired of that, Kershawn pulled Jeremy up to a sitting position and started punching him hard as fuck in the face. He broke his right-eye socket, his nose, and bloodied his mouth. Holding the front of his shirt, Kershawn grabbed a handful of his nuts, squeezing them. The pressure caused Jeremy to holler out in agony.

With a grunt, Kershawn hoisted him over his head and body-slammed him upon the kitchen table. The kitchen table broke and sent splinters flying everywhere. Jeremy lay where he was, groaning in pain. Kershawn grabbed him by his leg, and dragged him over to the center of the floor. Straddling him, he went to work on his face, rearranging shit and dotting his clothes with his blood.

When Kershawn had gotten done with pounding Jeremy's face, he leaned away from him, breathing heavily. He wiped his bloody brass knuckles on his shirt, and stuck them inside his jacket's pockets. He pulled out an ink pen and the divorce paperwork, lying them down beside Jeremy.

"Alright, Mr. Bevol, I need you to sign those documents I laid on the floor beside you. Once you're done, I'll drop that paperwork off to your future ex-wife, and you'll never have to see me again. Well, that is if you keep your mouth shut about this lil' altercation between you and I. Do we have a deal?" Kershawn asked Jeremy as he lay barely conscious. Jeremy groaned from a throbbing headache and an aching face. He nodded slightly and spat two broken, bloody teeth on the floor. "Okay, then, gon' and gemme your John Hancock." He picked up the ink pen and placed it into Jeremy's hand. He then got off of him, watching him turn over on his side and put his signature on all of the necessary documents. Once he was done, Kershawn thanked him, folded the paperwork up, and slid it back inside of his jacket. He thanked Jeremy for his cooperation and stomped his crotch. He hollered out in excruciation and grabbed himself, grimacing.

*That was the easiest two-hunnit bandz I've ever made. That mothafucka wasn't so tough! He was far from the gangsta attorney ol' girl warned me about. Hmmm, I bet he's one of those assholes who are only on that rah, rah shit with women. He's all bark and no bite when it comes to men, ol' soft-ass nigga. I should roll back up in there and finish whipping off in his ass,* Kershawn thought as he made his way across the living room, towards the front door. He was ignorant of the fact that Billie had been watching him through the window the entire time. The way he was carrying on, she thought he was going to beat Jeremy to death, but he stopped himself short.

***

Billie hopped the picket white fence and hauled her ass down the sidewalk. She ran out into the street, opened the backdoor of her uncle's car and climbed inside. Once she slammed the door shut, she crawled back inside the trunk and pulled the seat back up. She couldn't believe what she had witnessed. From what she'd pieced together, her Uncle Kershawn was the muscle for some organized crime syndicate, probably the mafia.

*So, that's how he makes his money. He's a goon. I knew he was doing something more than bouncing niggaz at clubs and after-hour spots. I don't understand why he couldn't just tell me that, though. It's notta big deal. I mean, it isn't like he's some kind of hit-man or some shit,* Billie thought, as she lay inside the trunk. Her train of thought was broken once she heard the driver's door open and her uncle get inside. He slammed the door shut and drove off. She overheard him call someone, making arrangements to meet up. She figured it had to have been the lady that had hired him to get those divorce papers signed. Afterwards, he disconnected the call, turned the volume up on some Aretha Franklin song, and crooned along with her.

### *Forty minutes later*

Billie stirred awake, hearing someone at the trunk. She rolled as far back inside of the trunk as she could. The trunk halfway opened and the light from the street lamp partially shone on her. Billie expected her uncle to discover that she was on board, but he didn't even look inside of the trunk. He just dumped his duffle bag inside of it and slammed it shut. The next thing she knew: he was getting back into the car and driving away. Billie could hear him surfing the airwaves for another oldie but goodie song. Once he found *Papa Was a Rollin' Stone* by The Temptations, he left the dial alone and started his routine of singing and driving.

Billie's curiosity had gotten the better of her. She was dying to find out what was inside the duffle bag. So she unzipped it and peered inside. Her eyes doubled in size, and her mouth flung open. There were several bankrolls of dead presidents inside, with rubber bands around them. She didn't know exactly how much money was inside the duffle bag. But by the looks of it, she gathered it was one hundred and fifty to two hundred thousand dollars.

*Man, unc's hand got hit with this kinda loot, just for going upside a nigga's head? Hell, I've been throwing them thangz since I was a shorty. I could do what he does. No problem,* Billie thought, as she zipped the duffle bag back up. She listened to old school song after old school, until she found her eyelids growing heavy and she yawned. She'd begun to doze off when she heard Kershawn's cell phone ringing over the music. Suddenly, the music was turned down low, and she could hear him chopping it up on his cellular.

"I'm on my way back to the crib, nigga. Why? What's up? Yeah, I can make that happen. You remember my quote, don't chu? Good. Just drop me the addy. No. You know I don't write shit down. I can memorize it—okay. I got it. Gemme, uhhhh, say, twenty-five minutes. Smooth. I'll holla at chu then. Peace." Kershawn disconnected the call and turned the music back up, singing along with it again. After hearing that conversation, Billie wondered what kind of mission her uncle was being sent on now. She figured he was going to beat someone up and earn himself another obscene amount of money. Now, she didn't know if that was for sure, but she sure as shit was going to find out. She couldn't help it. She was nosy. Not only that, she loved sneaking around, spying on him. It was definitely exciting. She got an adrenaline rush from it.

Twenty-five minutes later, Billie felt the car being pulled over. The music and the engine were murdered, but she could still hear Kershawn singing softly. From what she heard, he had popped open the glove-box and removed his gun and ski mask. A second later, he was hopping out of the car and slamming the door shut behind him. Billie waited five minutes before she let down the back seat and climbed out again. Peeking out of the back window, she saw Kershawn enter through the gate of a mint-green apartment complex. He walked up to the maintenance closet door and picked its lock. Once he finally had gotten it open, he went inside and returned shortly with an aluminum ladder. Kershawn carried the ladder over to the side of the tenement, disappearing from out of Billie's sight. Wondering what he was up to, she hopped out of the car and shut the door gently. She opened the gate of the complex, and darted over to the side of it, peering around the corner of it. She watched as her uncle, who was standing at the very top of the ladder, pulled out a glass-cutter and latched it on the window. Carefully, he used the chisel of the tool to carve a circle the size of a saucer into the window's glass. Once he released the glass he'd carved out of the window, he stashed the glass-cutter inside his jacket.

Kershawn snaked his arm inside the hole he'd cut out, and unlocked the window from the inside. He pushed the window open, pulled out his gun and climbed inside the window. Billie climbed up the ladder and looked through the window. She saw through the bathroom. Kershawn was chasing after a tall, lanky nigga rocking an unkempt afro with a natural fork in it. The man was covered in beads of water, and a pink towel was wrapped around his waist. He was heading right for the large window that resided over the living room couch. Abruptly, the lanky nigga dove like he was going inside of a swimming pool. The window exploded as he went flying through, bringing broken glass along with it. Billie's eyes bulged, and her mouth hung open. She couldn't believe her eyes.

Billie climbed halfway down the ladder before jumping down to the ground. She landed on her bending knees and took off running, bending the corner of the complex. As she neared the front of the apartment building, she saw the lanky nigga run across her line of vision. He was running so fast that his towel flew away from his body, leaving him completely naked. His upper body was covered in small bloody cuts from crashing through the window. On top of that, his hair was sparkling from the particles of glass in his afro. The lanky nigga opened the gate and bolted down the sidewalk, bare feet smacking against the pavement. Kershawn was right on his ass, clutching his gun tightly as he chased after him. He had run right across Billie, but hadn't noticed her standing there. His main concern was the tall, lanky nigga. He had his sole attention, so he wasn't thinking about anyone else.

"Helllllp! Someone help meeeee! He's tryna kill me, man! He's tryna kill me!" The lanky nigga yelled over and over again, occasionally looking over his shoulder at Kershawn. He was trying to see how close he was on him. Sadly for him, the professional hit-man was slowly beginning to close the distance.

Seeing what was going on, Billie darted out of the gate of the complex and followed her uncle. She chased after him, as he chased after the man he intended to kill. She saw the lanky nigga make a right and get swallowed by the darkness of an alley. Her uncle was swallowed by the darkness next. Billie would go on to be the third of them that was swallowed up. As soon as she entered the alley, she saw her uncle get down on one bending knee and extend his gun. He clutched it with both hands, and angled his head slightly to the side. From the way he was positioning himself, she could tell he was taking aim at homeboy fleeing from him. And the longer he waited to open fire, the wider the distance between them was becoming, and the smaller the window of opportunity was shrinking.

Billie snuck over to a big green trash bin and kneeled down behind it. She was only ten feet away from her uncle. She poked her head out from the side of the van, and continued to watch him. His arms jerked slightly as he pulled the trigger of his gun twice. His hushed bullets ripped through the air, back to back, heading toward their mark. The first bullet ripped through his victim's calf muscle and broke the bone. The second bullet did the same to his other calf. Billie heard the lanky nigga holler out in excruciation and flop to the ground of the filthy alley. He lay on his stomach, trying to crawl forward and calling out for help. Kershawn stood upright and ran down the alley after him. He kicked him over onto his back and listened to his pleas of mercy. Next, he leveled his gun at his heart, popping one in his beating heart, and two in his forehead. As wisps of smoke came from out of the silencer on the barrel of his gun, Kershawn lowered it beside him and took the time to examine his handiwork.

Seeing it was time she distanced herself from the situation, Billie made to run and ended up knocking over an empty can of peaches. The clinking of the can falling, alerted Kershawn to Billie's presence. As soon as he laid eyes on her, he chased after her. She ran towards the end of the alley she'd come from. Kershawn stopped running and lifted his gun. He tried to draw a bead on her, but she started zig zagging down the alley.

"Fuck!" Kershawn cussed and lowered his gun, continuing his chase after Billie. Billie cleared the threshold of the alley with him right on her heels. Although she was fast on her feet, Kershawn had stamina on his side and was just as fast. Shortly, Billie found herself hot, sticky and out of breath. She occasionally looked over her shoulder at her uncle. He was getting closer and closer, closing the distance between them exceptionally fast.

Kershawn ran upon the trunk of a parked car, and took long strides across the roofs of other vehicles lined up on the block. He kept his eyes locked on Billie as he timed his jumps. He came down upon the hood of an old Cadillac Deville, and leaped off of it. Looking at the ground as she ran, Billie could see her uncle's shadow eclipsing her. When she looked over her shoulder at him, he came crashing down on top of her. Billie winced as they collided with the ground. The fall had knocked the wind out of her, and it hurt like hell.

Scowling, Kershawn turned Billie over onto her back and stuck his gun underneath her chin. He was about to pull the trigger when he recognized her. "Billie? What the fuck are you doing here? You're supposed to be at home." His face frowned up behind the ski mask. Hearing the police cars' sirens as the cops were heading to their location, Kershawn understood that he and his niece had best get the fuck out of there. He had a hot gun in his hand, and a dead body he was responsible for not too far away. With that in mind, Kershawn grabbed Billie's hand and they ran back toward his car. Along the way, he flung his gun aside and kept on running. Once they'd gotten back inside of his whip, Kershawn fired it up and took off like a bat out of hell. The wheels of his vehicle squealed as he bent the corner in a hurry, and sped down the street.

\*\*\*

Billie sat before Kershawn's desk inside his study. He was busy down on his knees at the digital safe he had in the floor. The duffle bag he'd collected for that night's licks was sitting beside him. He was taking his time tossing the bankrolls inside of the safe without counting them. In all of his years of being in the murder game, no one that had ever acquired his services had tried to short change him. He figured it was because they knew that he would go hard behind his, no matter the amount. Once Kershawn had finished loading his safe with the money for the jobs he'd pulled that night, he shut his safe's door and tossed the empty duffle bag upon his desk top. He then plopped down in the seat of his executive officer chair, and focused his attention on Billie, placing the tips of his fingers together.

"So how do you feel knowing what I really do for a living now?" Kershawn asked her.

Billie shrugged and said, "Nothing really. It's a job like any other job, I guess. I mean, you make enough money to take good care of us, and that's all that really matters to me. The people you hurt aren't innocent, are they?" she inquired. If they weren't innocent then she could deal with it, but if they were, she couldn't respect her uncle's hustle.

"Nah, rest assured I have never given it to someone who didn't have it coming. The niggaz I handle are either some shady mothafuckaz, or some fools that are in the lifestyle."

"What about that nigga you knocked off his feet tonight? What was his story?"

"That asshole was an orderly at an old folks' home. He was stealing from the residents there and beating up niggas' grandmas and grandpas. A nigga put in the order, and he got dealt with. It was as simple as that." Billie nodded her understanding.

50

"I want chu to teach me the game, unc." She gave him a stern look, letting him know that she meant business.

Kershawn frowned up and shook his finger inside of his ear, saying, "I'm sorry. Run that by me again."

"I said, '*teach me the game*'." She repeated with no problem.

Billie was as serious as a heart attack, and he could tell by the look on her face. "Baby girl, this isn't something you wanna get into. I'm telling you, if I had the chance to do it all over again, I'd—"

"With all due respect, unc, save me the lectures. Whether you train me or not, I'ma do my thing regardless. I'll just have to learn through trial and error, which may lead to my untimely death. Still, I am willing to risk it. But under your tutelage, I'd prosper much better in these streets."

Kershawn stared at Billie for a while, thinking things over. By the look in her eyes, he came to the conclusion that she wasn't going to budge on her decision. Her mind was made up. He could very well allow her to go behind his back and get involved in the murder game. But like she had said, that could lead to her death. Her best chance at survival was if he trained her and taught her the proper way to do things. Having come to his conclusion, Kershawn took a deep breath before speaking again.

"Okay, I'll take you on," Kershawn said. Billie smiled as she hopped up from her seat and ran over to him. She hugged him and kissed him on the cheek affectionately, sitting on his knee. "Ain't none of that lovey dovey stuff gonna work with me, baby girl. I'm telling yo lil' ass now, if I don't feel like you're ready when the time comes, then we're staying up there until I feel you're at where you needa be. You hear?" He stared into her eyes and she smiled at him, nodding.

"Yes, Uncle Kershawn." Billie smiled broadly and hugged her uncle tight around his neck, kissing him on the cheek again. "I love you."

"I love you too, baby girl. Now get offa my leg, yo ass too big for this shit. You're notta baby no more." He tapped her on the lower half of her back and she hopped up, making her way over to the door. Stopping, she turned around to him, smiling excitedly.

"You know, I couldn't ask for a better man to raise me."

Kershawn blushed and said, "Goodnight, Billie."

"Goodnight, Uncle Kershawn." She walked out of the study, closing the door behind her.

Kershawn picked up a framed photograph of him and his brother, Dershawn, when they were eight-year-old boys. Looking at it, he took a deep breath and continued to study his brother's youthful face. "Bro, I bet chu are turning over in your grave right now, but I feel like I am making the right decision here." He kissed the portrait and sat it back down on his desk top. Afterwards, he poured himself a glass of cognac and indulged, while thinking of what was to come.

\*\*\*

*The next day*

Billie was lying in her bed with her headphones on, listening to music while writing inside her diary. The music was so loud in her ears that she couldn't hear someone rapping at her door. After a while of knocking and not getting an answer, the door opened and Kershawn stuck his head inside her bedroom. He waved his hand at Billie until he finally got her attention. She pulled her headphones down from her ears and sat up in bed, closing her diary.

"What's up, unc?" Billie asked.

Kershawn responded by entering her bedroom and shutting the door behind him. He walked over to her, and extended a book to her. Billie's face frowned up, looking at the strange-looking book. She could tell the book was old ass shit. It looked like it had been around for centuries, and it had. Billie sat her diary aside and took the book from her uncle, looking down at it. The old, thick, timeworn, cherry-brown book had a unique design engraved on its cover. The cover had a silver human skull with snakes coming out of its eye sockets, and swords forming an X behind it. There were rusted gold hinges at both ends of it, and a rusted latch with a padlock attached. The book had information about the art of murder that dated back to the medieval era, to the 1800s, until present day.

Every assassin that the book had been passed to, including its latest owner, placed new information inside of it. Its information was priceless to a professional killa. Kershawn took a necklace from around his neck that was held onto a golden skeleton key. He passed the key to Billie, and instructed her to use it to open the book. Billie used the key to unlock the padlock, and flipped the latch open. She opened the book to a beige, tattered page with a long list of rules dating back eons ago.

"How old is this thing?" Billie asked Kershawn while she flipped through the pages of the book.

"I can't give you a definite time, but from what I was told, that book has been around for eons," Kershawn informed her. "There is a vast amount of information in there on the human anatomy, the human psyche, war tactics and strategies, amongst other things."

"How'd you get your hands on it?" she asked curiously.

"That, young lady, is a story for another day, but I can tell you this—" Kershawn went on to tell Billie about the last five members of Loyalty Over Everything, aka The League of Executioners, L.O.E. for short. It turned out that there were only five members from Generation X left. And they all were in possession of a key that could open the very book that Billie held in her hands. He told her that one of the members had run afoul at a very powerful man that put a hefty bounty on their heads. The members had some of the top hit-men in the murder game looking for them. Two of them had been assassinated, so only three of them were still alive. This was thanks to them hatching a plan that made the powerful man back the fuck up off of them.

"So, that's what that ink stands for," Billie looked at the fading L.O.E tattoo on the side of his hand. He glanced at the tattoo and looked back up at her, nodding. "Where are they now?" she inquired about the surviving members of his order.

"They're around. Every few years we meet up for a drink and catch one another up on what's going on in our lives."

"That's what's up," Billie said, continuously flipping through the pages. "When do we start my training?"

"Once you finish that book, we'll start your physical training up in the mountains," Kershawn told her. "We'll stay up there for at least a year, getting you ready."

"Damn, unc, an entire year?" Billie frowned, feeling like that was a long time.

"Yes, an entire year. And watch yo mouth, young lady." He chastised her about cussing.

"My bad."

Kershawn looked at her with a tilted head and raised eyebrow. He hated when she used the phrase 'my bad' as an apology. To him that wasn't a proper apology. She knew this, but sometimes she forgot.

Billie sighed and said, "Okay, I'm sorry."

"Much better." Kershawn rose from the bed, kissed Billie on her forehead, and walked out of her bedroom, pulling the door shut behind him.

It took Billie three weeks to finish indulging in the book her uncle had given her. Once her reading was out of the way, Kershawn took her up to the mountains. There, he taught her how to defend herself and breathe in a fight. He even showed her how to calm herself when critically wounded, to slow her heart rate and blood flow so that she wouldn't bleed to death. Next, he demonstrated, with a pointer-stick, the areas of the human body to attack to kill a man quick and proficiently. He also showed Billie the proper way to wield a knife and use it as a weapon. Once the sixth month had approached and he was sure that she had devoured every lesson, he moved her on to guns.

By the time Billie had completed her year of training, she was at the peak level of *physically fit* for someone her age, and her body had developed a muscular tone. Not only was she stronger, but she was faster. Kershawn had turned her into a Super Billie. And she loved it.

*** 

Nightfall had captured the mountains by the time Kershawn and Billie got ready to leave the cabin. They loaded all of their belongings into the trunk of Kershawn's whip and hopped in, driving down the path of the woods. The drive back to the city was quiet, except for the soulful crooning of Al Greene playing from the stereo. Looking up at the green sign above the freeway, Kershawn saw they were nearing home, and that now would be the perfect time to spring his bit of knowledge on Billie.

Kershawn turned down the volume of his stereo and removed the manila envelope he'd placed in the flap of the sun-visor, when he'd gotten into the car. He nudged Billie with his elbow and passed her the manila envelope. She frowned up, wondering what her uncle could possibly be giving her.

"What's this?" Billie asked, as she opened the manila envelope. She removed a mug-shot photo and detailed information regarding the nigga in the picture. He was a chubby faced, African American man, with five cornrows and a five o'clock shadow. "Who's he?"

"Rico Bivens," Kershawn informed her. "He used to sell big time dope back in the day. Man ruled his neighborhood through intimidation and violence. He developed a fierce reputation over the years, thanks to his sheer brutality and the supreme dope his hustlers slung in the trenches."

"And?" Billie shrugged, like, *What's the big deal?* "What's he supposed to mean to me?"

Kershawn was silent for a minute. He could feel Billie's eyes on him as he took a breath. He was prepared to reveal the truth to her. He just hoped she received it well.

"Rico Bivens is the man that murdered your mother and father, Billie."

***

*"So, this is how this shit is gon' go," Rico spoke from the end of the kitchen table. He wore a homemade stocking cap over his frizzy cornrows, a black hefty hooded coat and gray Dickies. He had light-brown eyes, a scruffy beard that wouldn't grow on certain areas of his face, and a big black*

*mole on the side of his nose. "I've got two bags of dope here." He laid his chrome .45 automatic down upon the table top and pulled out two identical packets of dope. They both were stamped 'Pandemic', but there was a catch to them. "One is laced with poison while the other is pure heroin, homeboy. I'ma give you a choice of which one you wanna shoot up. The right one will leave yo ass high, and the wrong one will leave yo ass dead. Choose wisely." He tossed both packets of dope upon the table top.*

*Theresa cried and whimpered as she exchanged glances with Dershawn. Her entire body was trembling. She was completely terrified of what was about to occur. Dershawn was too, but he was trying to hold himself together for both of them.*

*"Don't worry, baby, don't worry, okay? Everything— everything is going to be fine." Dershawn reached over the table and grasped Theresa's hand, trying his best to comfort her.*

*"Yeah, baby, everything is gonna be fine—as long as you do like I say." Rico gave them a stern look, letting them know that he meant business and wasn't playing with their asses. "Now, choose." He extended his closed fists before Dershawn. In each one he had a packet of the dope. He was literally holding Life and Death in his hands. The feeling was euphoric, and made him feel like a god.*

*"No, no, no," Dershawn shook his head. "I can't do it! I won't do it! We can go about this another way, Rico. If you gemme some time I can pay you back for the heroin we stole." He assured Rico with a pleading look in his eyes.*

*"So, you're telling me you're not gonna pick one of these bags of dope, Dershawn?" Rico looked him in his eyes as he lowered his fists to the table top.*

"Look here, man, I don't mean no disrespect, but—" Dershawn's words were cut short, when Rico rolled his eyes annoyingly and nodded to one of his goons.

Blocka!

Theresa's head launched forward from the impact of a bullet. The back of her skull was smoking. It ricocheted off of the kitchen table and she fell to the floor, dead. The goon that delivered the kill-shot lowered his gun at his side and looked down at his handiwork. His eyes stayed focused on Theresa as he blew a big pink bubble out of his Bubble-Yum until it exploded. He then continued to chew his gum as Dershawn sobbed loudly, tears running down his face and green snot oozing out of his right nostril.

"You didn't—you didn't have to do that!" Dershawn cried aloud, looking at Rico like he wanted to rip his fucking head off. He knew better, though. By the time he would have reached Rico's end of the table, he and his goons would have chopped his ass down.

"I definitely did," Rico said seriously. "Lemme be clear, you're not in charge here. I am. The big black nigga with the gun is in charge. And I say you're gonna try your luck and pick one of these bags of Boy, or I'ma give my man behind you there the nod to pop yo skinny black ass!"

"Okay, okay, okay!" Dershawn told Rico, putting his hands up, giving in to his request. "I'll—I'll pick one." He studied Rico's fist for a moment, trying to figure out which fist he would pick. Making his mind up, he pointed to his left hand and Rico smiled devilishly.

"Excellent choice," Rico tossed the packet of dope he'd chosen before him. He then playfully drummed both of his hands on the table top. "Okay, now, where's the shit you use to shoot up with?" Dershawn told him where he could find the tools he used to shoot his heroin with. Rico sent one of *his goons off to get it. He returned with a worn, black leather case and sat it on the table top in front of Dershawn.*

*Dershawn looked back and forth between the leather case and Rico's scowling face. He always knew that he'd answer for his thievery one day. He just didn't expect it to come so soon. Dershawn opened the leather case and removed all of the items he'd need to cook up the heroin. Rico and his goons watched him closely as he drew up a shot, squirting just a little out of the needle of the syringe. He then slowly slid the needle into the bulging vein in his forearm as he balled his hand into a fist. Looking down at his vein, he rested his thumb on the plunger of the syringe. His heart thudded crazily. He was quite sure what to expect after injecting the dope into his body.*

*"My nigga, gon' handle yo business," Rico urged Dershawn, pointing his .45 automatic at him. He didn't feel any sympathy for the dope fiend. He was in his situation on account of him and his bitch stealing from him. The way he looked at it, there was a price to pay for taking his product, and he was looking to collect in full.*

*Dershawn looked at the blood inside the shaft of the syringe that had changed the heroin burgundy. He then looked up into that nigga Rico's face. The dope man had a pair of unforgiving eyes and clenched teeth, which caused his jaws to thump. Dershawn was looking for mercy, but he sure as hell wasn't going to get it from him. With that thought, he swallowed the lump of fear in his throat and pushed down on the plunger. A moment later, his eyes bulged and his mouth flew open. His heart raced out of control, and he clutched at the left side of his chest. Suddenly, his body went through a tantrum that threw him back in his chair. His arms and legs thrashed around, and his head shook violently. Foam poured out of the side of his mouth while blood ran out of his eyes, nose, and ears. Dershawn was jerking so hard and fast that he fell out of the chair and landed on the floor.*

*Thud!*

*Rico lowered his gun at his side as he watched Dershawn take his last death twitches. Without taking his eyes off of Dershawn's rigid form, Rico addressed his goons. "Y'all wanna know what the coldest part about this shit was?"*

*"What's that?" one of the goons asked.*

*Rico looked at him and said, "It didn't matter what bag this mothafucking dope fiend picked."*

*The goon frowned curiously. "Why is that?"*

*"Both of 'em were laced with poison," Rico confessed with a smile and tucked his .45 into the front of his Dickies.*

*The goon chuckled and said, "Youz a cold-ass nigga, Rico."*

*"That's the only way you gon' survive in this game, homeboy," Rico told him. "Y'all niggaz come on, man. I'm hungry as a hostage. Let's go get something to eat." With that said, Rico and his goons made their way out of the backdoor of the house, leaving the dead bodies of Dershawn and Theresa behind.*

\*\*\*

Kershawn glanced in Billie's direction to see how she'd taken the bombshell he'd dropped on her. By the look on her face, he could tell that she was shocked and confused. "You don't have anything to say?" he asked.

"Yeah. I thought this mothafucka been dead! As a matter of fact, you told me he and his boys got into a shoot-out with a rival drug crew and he was killed."

"I lied. I lied because I know you wouldn't be able to move on, knowing the man that smoked your parents was still alive. Now, with that said, I coulda been done slumped homeboy, but that wasn't my place. I figured you'd like to be the one who had the honor—seeing as how it was your parents he'd murdered." He glanced at her again, to find her nodding understandingly. He was right. She did want to be the one that killed Rico for taking her family away from her. Before, she was fine thinking that Kershawn had done the deed, but in the back of her mind, she wanted to be the one that settled the score. After all, it was her parents he had blown off the map.

"Look, kid, if you aren't up for the task, I could always go ahead and—" Billie cut Kershawn short, speaking with a distinct edge to her voice.

"Nah, unc, me and this mothafucka is gon' dance— tonight." Billie scowled, staring down at the mug shot of Rico.

***

Kershawn parked two houses down from Rico's crib. He kept his whip idling, but executed its headlights. He popped open the glove-box and removed a Beretta, a silencer, and a black ski mask. He placed everything on Billie's lap. She tucked the Beretta on her waistline, and stuck the silencer inside her pocket. Next, she pulled the ski mask down over her face and hopped out of the car, closing the door shut quietly. Hunched over, she moved towards the house of the man she intended to kill, making sure there weren't a pair of eyes watching her. She slipped over into the bushes, where she was sure no one would see her, and played the waiting game. Two hours later, the bright headlights of a Lincoln

Town Car pulled up into the driveway. All Billie could see was the burly silhouette of a man in the driver seat, but a gut feeling told her it was Rico. He reached for something in the sun-visor, and the garage door lifted up. Seeing her chance to get inside the house, Billie got upon her bending knees and watched the Lincoln Town Car drive in. She waited until the garage door was almost closed before she ran toward it, rolling inside the garage.

Billie listened as gospel music played loudly from the Lincoln Town Car. She could hear faint sounds of the burly man singing. Getting upon her knees, she made it over to the trunk of the boat-sized vehicle and stuck her head out from the side of it. Suddenly, the Lincoln's engine was killed and the driver's door was thrown open. A six-foot-three three-hundred-pound man stepped out of the Lincoln Town Car, one black leather shoe at a time. Once he stood at his full height, she took in his appearance and the expensive suit that fit him to the T. Rico was a mahogany-complexioned man with a shiny bald head, glasses and a thick graying beard. His suit was the color of a plum. He had on a violet tie and powder blue button-up shirt.

*Why is he crying?* Billie thought, as her face frowned up. She watched as Rico removed his glasses and used his handkerchief to dab his tearful eyes. Afterwards, he slid his glasses back on and grabbed his black leather briefcase from the backseat. He headed up the stairs, inside his house, and shut the door behind him. Rico crying wasn't a big deal at all for Billie. She figured his tears were on account of his being moved by the gospel music he was listening to. Billie had been to church a few times when she was a little girl. She'd witnessed a few fat women—and even a couple of men—catch the Holy Ghost and fall flat out in the aisles. That shit used to trip her out. She'd never caught it, and she'd never seen any kids catch it either. She figured all the adults were putting on a show. You know, trying to act like they were actually touched by the hand of God?

Pulling her Beretta from the small of her back, Billie screwed the silencer onto its barrel and crept over to the door. Gently, she twisted the knob and cracked the door open. Looking through the opening, she saw Rico moving around in the kitchen, singing the gospel song he'd been listening to in his car, and pouring himself a glass of cognac. He opened his black leather briefcase and pulled out his Bible. Opening the Holy book, he began to read a passage while taking casual sips of the strong liquor. Rico picked up his Bible, and made his way down the hallway, reading it. Billie crept inside the house and snuck her way down the hallway. She was sure to move as gracefully and as quietly as she could, so her prey wouldn't detect her. She utilized her stealth just like Kershawn had taught her.

She heard the door of the room Rico had entered click shut. Placing her back against the wall, she slid alongside it with her gun at her side. Stopping at the door her intended victim was behind, she tapped the trigger of her gun and its infra-red laser was activated. Billie was breathing heavily. Her face was sweaty behind the ski mask, and her heart was thudding. The anticipation of her first kill had her chest swollen with anxiousness. It seemed like she'd been waiting all of her life to finally claim vengeance for her parents' death. She'd dreamt of killing the man solely responsible for her growing up an orphan. And the time was at hand. The anticipation made her moist between her legs and her clit hard.

Billie's heart was thudding so loudly she could hear it in her ears. Taking a deep breath, she twisted the knob and flung the door open. Swiftly, she jumped into the doorway with both hands clutching her gun. She was aiming the red dot exactly where she wanted her bullet to go. Her brows furrowed, when she saw Rico sitting calmly at the desk of his study. He was wearing his black and purple clergy rope and scarf. His head was bowed, and his eyes were focused on the notepad he was writing on.

"Come in, I've been expecting you," Rico said without lifting his head, continuing to write. Cautiously, Billie made her way inside his study, swaying her gun around and checking around for any threats. Once she didn't find any, she focused her attention and her gun on Rico, who still wasn't paying her any mind. "Relax. There's no one here besides you and I. Like I told you, I've been expecting you."

"How the fuck did you know I was coming?" Billie asked him angrily. She'd initially thought he was talking out of his ass about knowing she was coming, but now she believed he really did know. The only other question she had in mind was how did he know?

"Lord Almighty told me you were coming, Billie Hoyle," Rico told her. "He told me a week in advance that you would pay a call upon me. That's why I took the liberty to act like I'd come down with the flu, when the time came for my family to fly out to Arkansas. You see, my father-in-law is celebrating his sixty-seventh birthday, and we were all going out there to spend the week with him. I couldn't go on account of me being ill. But I urged my wife and kids to go along. I didn't want you coming here to assassinate me while they were here. Seeing your loved one murdered in front of you will leave an emotional scar that can never be healed."

Billie was shocked to find out that Rico knew who she was, and that she was coming to claim his life. She started to think that maybe God was real. It wasn't like there was some other way to explain how he knew what he knew about her.

Still, she wasn't about to lower her guard. He could be laying a trap for her ass, and she wasn't about to get caught in one on her first mission. "If you knew I was coming here to kill you, why didn't you shake the spot? Or prepare to mount a defense or something? You mean to tell me that you're just gonna lay down and die?" Billie asked with narrowed eyelids. She found it hard to believe that he was just going to let her kill him. Self-preservation was one law that mankind never broke. So, she found his reasoning odd.

Rico took the time to fold up the letter he'd written. He placed it inside an envelope, and licked it shut. He then laid it on top of two other envelopes which were addressed to his children. The letter he'd just finished was his longest, and it was addressed to his beloved wife. Picking up his glass of cognac, Rico lay back in his executive office chair, and gave Billie his undivided attention. Billie studied him closely. He didn't seem fearful or worried at all. She expected him to be cowering and begging for his life. But he wasn't doing either. She had to tip her hat to him. He was one courageous mothafucka.

"I've done more wicked in my lifetime than I care to remember," Rico began with his explanation. "I've spent the last thirty years trying to atone for my evil deeds because I was sure my day of reckoning was coming. Whether you right your wrongs or not, you've still gotta pay for the bad you've done. No matter how long ago it was. I've already accepted my fate, and I've made my peace with God." Rico swallowed the last of the alcohol in his glass, and sat it on the desk top. He then grabbed his rosary as he stood upright, and looped it over his head. He took the time to adjust his robe. Then, he held his head high and stuck his chest out. He wore a stern expression as he prepared to meet his end. "I'm ready when you are. I'd like to ask that you grant my dying wish, if you don't mind, of course."

"Spit it out," Billie said without remorse.

"Don't shoot me in the face. I'd like for my family to have an open casket funeral for me." He said this shit like he was asking for a glass of water at someone's house. You would have never thought he was in the position to be killed at this moment. The former dope man was really okay with leaving this world for the next.

"I got chu faded," Billie told him.

"Thank y—" Before Rico could finish his sentence, Billie hit his big ass with two shots to the heart. His eyes bulged behind the lenses of his glasses, and his mouth flung open. He staggered backwards and fell. Billie approached him, kicking his foot to see if he'd move. When he didn't budge, she checked his pulse and confirmed his death. Afterwards, she took a breath, turned out the desk light on his desk top, and exited his study, shutting the door behind her.

\*\*\*

Billie hopped into the front passenger seat and slammed the door shut. Kershawn pulled away from the curb, and drove down the residential block as though his niece didn't just catch a body. He looked back and forth between the windshield and Billie, trying to read the look on her face.

"You good? You handled that?" Kershawn asked.

"Yeah, it's done," Billie assured him. "You know I was expecting to feel some kind of relief. But truthfully, nothing has changed. I still feel the same."

"Oh, yeah, how exactly do you feel?"

"Angry—" Billie confessed. Her voice cracked emotionally, and tears slid down her cheeks. "And—and hurt—" The floodgates opened, and her face was drenched. Her body shook uncontrollably. Kershawn quickly pulled over the car and put it in park, leaving it idling. He grabbed Billie and pulled her close to him, hugging her affectionately. He listened as she sobbed and shook in his arms. He rubbed her back soothingly, and kissed her on top of the head.

"Shhhhh, there, there now," Kershawn spoke in a calm soothing voice. "In time things will get better. You've just gotta take it one day at a time—one day at a time. You hear me?" Billie said *yes*. "I got you, and you got me. I love you, Billie. I love you more than life itself."

Billie continued to shake and sob in her uncle's arms. He held her tighter and continued to console her, as tears slowly collected in his eyes and rolled down his cheeks.

# Chapter 3

## 2015

The sun shone brightly through the rectangle windows of the double doors of Horace Mann middle school. It was ten o'clock in the morning, and Billie was mopping the hallway, leaving wet streaks behind. Billie was wearing a navy blue Dickie jumpsuit, with an identification badge hanging from her breast pocket. An assortment of keys that granted her access to every door of the school hung from the belt loop of her suit. Billie had her ear-buds in her ears, and was nodding her head to Lil' Wayne's *Visine* as she performed the task assigned to her. She moved down the corridor, gripping the mop's handle and swaying it from left to right. Billie was so engrossed in her music that she didn't hear her supervisor calling her name over and over again. It wasn't until he pulled out his whistle and blew it that he'd garnered her attention. Billie removed one of her earphones from out of her ear, and looked up at her supervisor, Mr. Hogan, like, *What's up?*

"Billie, I need to holla at chu for a second," Mr. Hogan said. He was a five-foot-eight African American man, a shade lighter than she was. He had a small salt-and-pepper afro and mustache. Right now, he was wearing a light gray pocket T-shirt; fitted stone-washed jeans and boots. His identification badge hung from one of his belt loops, while a large assortment of keys hung from the other. Mr. Hogan was a firm, but fair man that didn't take any shit off of anyone, regardless of whom they were or associated with.

Billie removed the earphone from her other ear and pulled out her iPod, wrapping the earphones' cord around it and then stashing it inside her back pocket. She then dunked the mop inside the bright yellow bucket, pushed it aside and sat out the wet floor sign. Once she'd done this, she followed Mr. Hogan inside his office, where he offered her a seat before his desk. Hesitantly, Billie sat down. She watched as Hogan looked over a stack of paperwork, as she fidgeted with her fingers. She wondered what he wanted with her.

Suddenly, Mr. Hogan took a deep breath and shook his head, having finished looking over the paperwork. He sat back in his chair, resting his hands in his lap, and crossing his booted feet on top of the desk. His eyes lingered on Billie, as he swallowed the spit in his throat before addressing her.

"Normally, we do background checks here at the LAUSD, but when I first hired you I had a feeling that you'd pass the B.G check with no problem. I mean, you didn't look like you've been in as much shit as they've got listed, but unfortunately you have." Billie raised an eyebrow, wondering what he was getting at. Having made note of this, Mr. Hogan picked up the stack of papers and tossed them down on the desk top before her. Quickly, she picked up the documents and began reading over them. "Anyway, my curiosity got the best of me, and I decided to go ahead and run your background. I must say, you have a long line of shit listed that I never thought you'd be capable of, foolish of me to have judged a book by its cover."

Billie finished looking over the paperwork and tossed it back down upon the desk, sitting back in her chair. "Exactly what are you getting at, John?"

"LAUSD doesn't take on convicted felons, so unfortunately, I'm gonna let chu go. You can finish up today, but—"

"Mr. Hogan, I need this job, I got so many bills that's coming up that I gotta pay. Christmas is coming up, and I need this gig to get my daughter gifts."

Mr. Hogan bowed his head and took a deep breath. He then looked up in her eyes and said, "I'm sorry, Billie, I really am. But this situation is outta my hands. I've got rules I have to follow by. We cannot have convicted felons working on the board. I hope you understand. I do apologize."

Billie shot up from her chair and said, "You know what, you can take your apology and shove it up yo ass!"

Billie stormed out of Mr. Hogan's office, putting on her ear-buds and playing Kelis' *Caught Out There*. She ran down the hallway and kicked over the yellow mop bucket, sending water splashing everywhere, coating the floor. Nearing the double doors of the exit, she jumped up in the air and kicked one of them open. As soon as the door flung open, she was engulfed by the radiant sun and met with the chirping birds, while the song kept playing in the earphones:

*I hate you so much right now*
*I hate you so much right now*
*Ah*
*I hate you so much right now*
*I hate you so much right now*

Billie popped the trunk of her '95 Honda Accord and grabbed the baseball bat that she had stashed inside. Patting the baseball bat in her palm, she scanned the parking lot for Mr. Hogan's car. An evil smile spread across her lips, when she spotted his money green old school Chevrolet Nova on original rims and tires. Billie ran over to the vintage vehicle and jumped on the hood of it, beating in its windshield until it cracked into a spider's cobweb. She then banged dents into the roof of the car, knocked off its side view mirrors, and thrashed the hood until its hood caved in.

"Punk-ass mothafucka! I told you this was the only way my baby can eat, but chu didn't give a fuck! So, guess what? I don't give a fuck either! You and the mothafucking school board can suck my big, black dick!" Billie jumped back down onto the asphalt, and made her way around the Chevrolet, busting out the windows. As soon as the glass windows were busted, shards rained down to the pavement, looking like twinkling diamonds as they lay there littering the ground.

Having grown exhausted from fucking up Mr. Hogan's car, Billie dropped her arms at her sides, still holding the baseball bat. As she took in the damage of the Chevy, Billie breathed huskily. Beating the shit out of Mr. Hogan's car made her feel a little better, but she still had financial problems to worry about.

Billie wiped the sweat that dripped from the corner of her brow. She then looked around to find several students and their teachers looking through the windows of their classrooms. Some of the students waved at Billie, and she cracked a smile, waving back. She then walked back over to her car, and tossed her baseball bat inside the trunk, slamming it shut. Billie had just jumped behind the wheel of her Honda, when Mr. Hogan ran out of the building into the parking lot. As soon as he saw how fucked up his was, he gripped either side of his head. Tears were in his eyes, and his bottom lip quivered. Wetness slid down his cheeks, as he walked around his old school Chevrolet, taking in the damage of his vehicle. He loved his car more than he loved his wife and three kids.

"I'ma kill you, bitch! I'ma fucking kill you!" Mr. Hogan pulled his keys from out of his pocket and ran to the trunk of his car, unlocking it. He threw the trunk open and snatched out the tire-iron, practicing swinging it. With a crazed look in his eyes, Mr. Hogan looked around the parking lot for Billie's Honda. When he spotted it, he went running at it, just as she was pulling out of her parking space. "Bitch, get back here! Get back here!"

Billie adjusted her side view mirror as she drove towards the exit of the parking lot. She saw her reflection in the side view mirror, as well as Mr. Hogan chasing after her. She watched as he hurled obscenities at her while striking the side of her whip repeatedly, knocking dents in the side of it. Billie mashed the gas pedal and sped off. He ran after her vehicle, and threw his tire-iron at it. The tire-iron ricocheted off the trunk of the Honda, and made a ringing noise when it landed into the street. Billie looked into her rearview mirror at Mr. Hogan, watching him grow smaller and smaller in the middle of the street. She stuck her hand out of the window, and held up the middle finger at him.

***

Billie drove inside the liquor store parking lot, and killed the engine of her Honda, jumping out. She slammed the door of her vehicle behind her, and made her way towards the entrance of the store, slipping on her jacket. She passed a thug-ass-looking nigga and his girl coming out of the store. The dude had a Black & Mild tucked behind his ear, and a bottle of something concealed in a wrinkled brown paper bag. They were talking to each other, moving past Billie as if she was invisible.

*Ding, dong!*

A bell chimed as Billie crossed the threshold of the liquor store. She went straight up to the graffiti-covered bullet-proof glass that separated the cashier from the patrons. Billie found a forty-something-year-old cashier with his legs kicked up on the counter, as he read a sleazy magazine. He was so engrossed in his magazine that he didn't noticed Billie standing before the glass. It wasn't until she knocked on the bullet-proof glass that he took notice of her. He sat the magazine aside and stood to his booted feet, scratching underneath his salt-and-pepper beard.

"What can I get chu, sweetheart?" the cashier, Ned, asked Billie.

"Yeah, gemme a pack of Newport 100s and, uhhh, fifth of Hennessy," Billie gave him her order. While he busied himself getting down what she'd asked for, Billie reached inside her pocket and pulled out a handful of dollars. She took her time straightening out the money she needed to pay for her items. Once the wrinkled bills were as straight as she could get them, she slid them inside the tray after Ned told her how much everything was. Ned gave *her* her change, and placed her bagged items inside a bullet-proof box that had a double sided door. Billie took her bag of items out of the box, thanked Ned and made her way out of the liquor store.

*** 

When Billie came through the door of her modestly decorated apartment, she found her four-year-old daughter, Annabelle, eating a big ass bowl of Fruit Loops and watching PJ Masks, with a couple of naked dolls scattered around her. Annabelle was a caramel-complexioned girl with freckles and auburn hair. She was dressed in a Sponge Bob T-shirt, jeans and socks. As soon as she saw her mother, her eyes grew big, and a big smile stretched across her face, displaying her top row of missing teeth.

Normally, Billie didn't leave her daughter home alone, but she didn't have enough time to drop her off at her Uncle Kershawn's house. She was running late for work, and if she was late one more time this week, she was told she'd be fired. So before she left out that morning, she told Annabelle to lock the door, and to not open it for anyone. She knew it was a bad idea to leave her daughter at home alone, but she was a single mother, and she was doing the best that she could on her own.

"Mommyyyy!" Annabelle jumped to her feet, running towards her mother.

"Heyyy, pretty girl!" Billie sat her bag of goods on the kitchen table. She was wearing a big smile when she scooped her baby girl up into her arms, kissing her all over her face, making her giggle and laugh. Once she was finished showing her affection, she sat her back down and pinched her cheek. "Hey, lil' mama, what chu doing? You miss me?"

"Watching cartoons—of course, I missed you, mommy. Did you miss me?" Annabelle asked jovially, dancing around, like little kids do. It was as though she couldn't keep still.

"You better believe it, kid," Billie said, smiling. She grabbed her and laid her on the couch, tickling her and kissing her on the side of the face. Annabelle laughed and giggled, which caused her to fart.

"Ewwww, that's yo stinky butt?" Billie frowned up, pinching her nose and fanning the air. She didn't really smell anything. She was just playing around with her daughter.

"Oops, my bad." Annabelle laughed and giggled again.

"Gemme a kiss, big head." Billie leaned over the arm of the couch and puckered up her lips. Annabelle leaned forward, giving her mother an Eskimo kiss, and then kissing her on the lips.

"Thank you, pretty girl," Billie said.

"You're welcome." Annabelle went back to eating her big bowl of cereal and watching cartoons.

Billie smiled hard on her way to the bathroom, clutching her bag of Hennessy. She entered the bathroom, flipping on the light switch and shutting the door behind her. The smile disappeared from her face, and she placed her back against the wall, sliding down to the floor on her bending knees. Billie made an ugly face as she cried, her body trembling hard. Tears pooled in her eyes and splashed on the tiled floor. Sitting the bag down on the floor beside her, she reached inside her back pocket, pulling out a folded up paper. She unfolded it and looked at it. It was an eviction notice to pay or quit. Billie's tears splashed on the paper, as she looked it over again. She had thirty days to come up with the money, or she was fucked. She and Annabelle would be thrown out in the streets.

Billie wept as she slammed the back of her head against the wall repeatedly. She then placed her hands against her face and ran them downward, exhaling. Billie grabbed her Hennessy, which was still inside the bag, and stood before the medicine cabinet mirror, looking at herself. Her eyes were pink and her nose was red. Teardrops fell from her eyes, dripping inside the porcelain sink.

Billie took note of her appearance, minus the bags forming under her eyes and the redness of her nose. She was a fairly attractive woman, with an athletic build and just the right amount of ass and tit. Little mama was drop-dead gorgeous. And on top of that, she was just as skilled with a mop as she was with a gun. You see, Billie or Billie Badass, as her peers in the underworld liked to refer to her as, was a hit-woman from the Westside of Compton.

Holding the gaze of her reflection, Billie removed the cap from her brown bottle of liquor. She took it to her head, guzzling it, spilling some of it down her chin. Billie wanted her worries to go away as soon as possible, and this was the only way she knew how to do that. She could smoke crack like her parents used to, but she saw first-hand what that shit did to you, and she didn't want any part of it. Besides, her old man had a circulatory overload fucking with crack, and a dope boy had killed her mother for stealing his work. Billie definitely didn't want to end up like that. She wanted better for herself and her daughter.

*"Look at chu, bitch, you're a fucking mess. Sitting up in here crying like a ho, while lil' mama in the living room, eating cereal, watching TV. That baby depends on you each and every day to provide and protect her. And now you wanna cry and shit 'cause shit getting rough. This is yo life, so woman the fuck up! If God didn't think a bitch as bad as yo'self couldn't get through these hard times, then he wouldn't be putting you through them."* After digesting those words her inner voice said to her, Billie tilted the Hennessy bottle downward, emptying its contents out into the sink, watching the alcohol swirl down the drain. Once she was done, she placed the empty bottle back inside the brown paper bag. Billie then looked at herself in the mirror, gripping either side of the porcelain sink. She bowed her head and took a deep breath, pulling herself together. Once she'd finally gotten a hold of herself, she opened the bathroom door and entered the living room. She was taken aback once she saw her daughter, Annabelle, playing with Kershawn, who was sitting in the reclining chair.

Although Kershawn was well into his fifties, he still had an impeccable shape and a well-fit body. Time had been kind to the old man. These days, instead of cornrows, he rocked a hairstyle similar to Fredrick Douglas, and an untamed, graying beard. The light-gray suit he was wearing fit him to the T. His attire made him look more like a lawyer from the 1800s than an ex hit-man turned contractor.

"Boyyyy, you done gave yo uncle a workout, makes me remember my age." Kershawn stood upright and pulled his handkerchief from out of his suit's breast pocket, dabbing the beads of sweat from off his forehead.

"You all right, Uncle Kershawn?" Annabelle asked him, holding his hand.

"Yeah, I'm okay," he responded, tucking the handkerchief back inside his breast pocket.

"Kershawn, how'd you get in here?" Billie asked him, as she held the bottle of Hennessy behind her back. She didn't want him to know that she'd been drinking; otherwise, he'd know that something had been troubling her. Billie had never been a drinker or a smoker, but hard times had driven her to pick up both as a vice.

"The beautiful young lady let me in," Kershawn pinched Annabelle's cheek affectionately, causing her to chuckle.

"Annabelle, I told you about opening up the door." Billie looked at her daughter disappointedly. When she looked at her offspring, the girl dropped her head shamefully.

"I'm sorry, mommy. It was Uncle Kershawn, though." Annabelle fidgeted with her fingers.

"I know, but what if it wasn't Uncle Kershawn? What if it had been someone tricking you, so they could get inside our home, huh?" Billie lifted up her daughter's chin so that she'd be looking into her eyes.

"You're right. I'm sorry, mommy." She looked at her mom with puppy dog eyes and a pouty bottom lip.

Billie took a deep breath. She loved her daughter dearly. Little mama was her Kryptonite. So when she looked at her with that saddening look, she softened up like ice near a fire. "Okay, all is forgiven. Now, why don't chu go into your bedroom and watch television while I talk to your uncle."

"Okay, mommy." Annabelle lightened up and smiled. She hugged her mother around the neck. She then walked over to Kershawn, kissing him on the cheek, and then hugging him around his neck. He smiled and patted her back affectionately. "Bye, mommy, bye Uncle Kershawn, I love you both." She ran out of the living room, shutting the door behind her.

"I love you too, sweetheart," Kershawn called after her. He then took the bottle of Hennessy from behind Billie's back, looking it over. "If you're drinking Henny straight, then you've hit a new low. Talk to me now, what's going on?" Kershawn sat beside Billie where she sat on the couch. She hunched over with her hands dangling between her legs, head bowed.

"I got fired today, unc." Billie ran her hand down her face and took a deep breath.

"For what?" Kershawn questioned with concern.

"Them mothafuckaz found out that I'ma felon. You know the school board doesn't want any dealings with no fucking felons. Fuck, man!" She slammed her fist on the arm of the couch, frustrated. No matter how many steps she took forward, she felt like she was taking even more back. She hated the struggle that came with trying to live a square life. She wasn't used to it. Nah, she was used to getting hers the illegal way: murder for hire. Back then, things were easier for her. She loved what she did, and it came easy to her. One pull of a trigger, her target was dead, and she was picking up a twenty-five thousand to fifty-thousand-dollar bag. Those days were long gone now though. She'd chosen to make her dough the legal way.

Billie paced the floor with her hands held behind her back, thinking. Kershawn sat the bottle of Hennessy down on the coffee table. He pulled a pack of Zig-Zags from out of his breast pocket, and a small transparent bag of tobacco from inside his suit. He went about the task of rolling up as he listened to his niece vent her grievances.

"I've gotta shit loada bills I've gotta pay at the end of this month. And what I get paid from the board isn't going to be enough to cover everything. On top of that, Christmas is on my ass. You know I don't have shit for lil' mama besides this punk ass tree?" She motioned to the little Christmas tree in the corner of the living room. It was white with decorations on it. The colorful lights surrounding it blinked on and off. There wasn't a gift under the small tree. That bitch was naked.

"You don't have anything put up?" Kershawn asked her, as he sprinkled the tobacco inside the white rolling paper.

"Man, I got less than a C-note to my name. The rest of my money I gave to Joaquin's attorney for his case. Fucking attorneys are vampires, unc, they suck you dry." She plopped down on the reclining chair, staring up at the ceiling with tears in her eyes.

"You ain't gotta tell me. You remember I nearly spent a quarter of a million dollars fighting that murder beef I had back in the day. Them janky mothafuckaz' pockets have a bottomless pit." With that said, he licked the rolling paper closed and pulled out a gold jukebox Zippo lighter. "Listen, I can float chu some cash until you get back on yo feet. Don't worry. You don't have to pay me back. We're family. We look out for our own." He put the blue flame to the tip of his homemade cigarette. He took a few drags of it and blew out a big ass cloud of smoke. Next, he pulled out his checkbook and a fountain pen. He sat them both on the coffee table, and slid them before Billie. "Write down whatever dollar amount you think you'll need. It's all on me."

Billie blinked back tears and then sat up on the reclining chair, saying, "Unc, you know I don't do handouts. A bitch makes her own way."

"I can respect that. I don't know why my old ass even offered you a dollar, knowing well you'd be too stubborn to take it." He leaned forward and passed her his cancer stick. As he blew out smoke from his nose and mouth, he tucked the checkbook and fountain pen away, where he'd pulled them out from. He then slumped on the couch, watching Billie indulge in the tobacco. "So, if you're not gonna take any of my coins, what're you gonna do about money?"

"To tell you the truth, I really don't know." She hit the stick a couple of times before passing it back to him. "I need a large sum of dough real fast. And working some square ass job isn't gonna gemme that. So whatever I dive head first into is definitely gonna be illegal."

"I thought you were done with the criminal lifestyle once you had lil' mama."

"I was, but I gotta child that's counting on me, and I can't let her down. A bitch gotta do what a bitch gotta do. Momma gotta make a way, you feel me?"

Kershawn tugged on his nappy beard as he thought about something. He then looked to Billie and said, "You ever think about getting back into the game?"

"You mean the—" she made her hand into the shape of a gun, and pointed it at him.

"Yeah, the murder for hire business."

"Shiiit, if the money is right, anybody can get it. At this point, I don't give a fuck." She took the cigarette from him and crossed her feet on top of the coffee table, indulging in the smoke. "What's up? You got an assignment for me?"

"Ain't nothing came up yet, but once it does I'll slide it yo way, if you tryna get down." He looked at her and waited for her response. He could tell that she was thinking on it as she sucked on the end of the tobacco stick, blowing out big clouds of smoke.

"Yeah, you can shout me a holla the moment something comes across yo desk."

"Alright, I'll keep you in mind." He spared a glance at his plain face Rolex watch. "Listen, I got some business I've gotta attend to, so I'ma cut outta here." Billie sat up on the chair and tried to pass him his stick back. He waved her off. "Nah, you hold on to that. That's yours."

"Good looking out."

"I'ma say goodbye to baby girl," Kershawn told her before heading to Annabelle's bedroom. He hugged her and gave her a kiss goodbye. He was about to walk away, until she reminded him that he owed her a dollar from the last time he'd come over. Smiling, he reached inside his pocket and pulled out a money-clip, removing a five-dollar bill. He gave it to her, saying, "Here you go, baby girl. This should hold you over 'til the next time I see you."

"Wow! Five big ones." Annabelle held the bill with Abraham Lincoln on it between her small hands, staring at it admiringly. "Oh, thank you, Uncle Kershawn." She hugged him and planted kisses all over his face.

"You're welcome, sweetheart. Be a good girl now."

"Okay."

Kershawn walked out of her bedroom, leaving the door open behind him.

"You gon' spoil my baby, you keep on giving her money all the time," Billie said with a grin on her face.

"That's all right, there's notta 'nough spoiled black children in this world."

"Amen to that shit." She snuffed out the ember of the stick inside the ashtray. She then turned to her uncle and opened her arms. "Gemme a hug, old man."

Kershawn smiled and hugged the niece he raised like a daughter. He then held her at arm's length and said, "Don't worry about anything. Everything is going to be okay. I'ma get chu this contract, and you gon' knock whomever this poor bastard is over. And you're gonna have more than enough money than you need to take care of things around here." He kissed her on the forehead and hugged her again. "I love you," he told her as he opened the front door to let himself out.

"I love you, too, unc," she replied before shutting the door behind him.

"Mommy, come watch *Powerpuff Girls* with me." Annabelle stuck her head out of her bedroom's door.

"Okay, Lil' Miss Bossy," Billie chuckled as she headed inside her daughter's bedroom. She sat down on the foot of the bed, and her daughter climbed into her lap. They watched cartoons together until they both eventually fell sound asleep.

Tranay Adams

# Chapter 4

## *That night*

Naked, Myron hung from the ceiling of a junky basement, with his wrists bounded by silver chains. His face was bloody, battered and bruised, while the rest of him was covered in bloody cuts. His left eyelid was swollen shut, so through his right eye, he followed God as he paced the basement floor. God had put two bad bitchez on Myron at the club. They drank and snorted coke with him. He was so shit-faced that he couldn't drive, so one of the girls did. They took him to a seedy motel in a really bad area of the city. The room only cost them fifteen bucks for four hours, and they'd stopped by a 24-hour liquor store to grab a bottle of Moët. The plan was to get drunk and high again, and spend the rest of their stay fucking. Unfortunately for Myron, he was so occupied making out with one girl that he neglected to pay attention to the other. While he was busy with her partner in crime, the other girl slipped an Ambien into Myron's flute of champagne. He drank it down. The next thing he knew: he was waking up to getting his ass whipped, and then he was suspended from a basement's ceiling.

"Now, normally, a boss-ass nigga such as myself wouldn't get his hands dirty—But this is beyond business here—You see, this shit here is personal!" God said, as he grabbed Myron by the lower half of his face and made his lips to pucker up. Blood oozed out of that nigga's mouth and slid down God's gloved hand. His goons, nicknamed God's Angels, watched him attentively from the shadows of the basement. "You and yo punk-ass brother killed my wife, my mothafucking daughter's mother, so yo asses gotta pay." God's eyebrows arched, and his nose scrunched up. He then clenched his jaws, which caused a vein on his temple to pulsate with animosity. He cocked back his gloved fist and fired on Myron's mouth, bloodying his grill. Myron's head launched backwards, and then it bowed again. He whimpered in pain, and dripped blood on the surface.

God walked away from Myron. While he strolled towards the center of the room, he pulled a golf club free from its bag. He then kicked the bag over, causing it to spill a dozen golf balls over the floor. God got into his stance, looking back and forth between the ball he had his eyes on and Myron. He practiced swinging his golf club at one of the balls, aiming it at Myron's face. Finally, he cocked his golf club high above his head, and swung it with all of his might. The golf club made a whacking sound as it impacted the ball. The hard white ball whistled through the air like a torpedo, heading for its target.

*Crack!*

The ball slammed into Myron's nose and indented it. Instantly, blood flooded his nostrils, and his eyes got as big as saucers. The pain was sharp and antagonizing. Myron threw his head back, screaming at the top of his lungs. God could see all the teeth inside of his mouth. It brought him a little comfort to cause pain to one of the men responsible for his wife's murder. Using his fist, God wiped the tears that dripped from the brims of his eyes. Although he should have been joyful in seeing Myron's suffering, thoughts of his late wife being gunned down in the streets were ruining the moment for him. Still, he had to push forward and give her the justice she deserved.

"It hurts, don't it, mothafucka? That pain you feeling right now, ain't shit compared to what my daughter and I felt the day you and yo' punk-ass brother snatched my wife from us." God focused his attention back on the golf ball, lining it up with the ball he had in mind. He cocked his golf club above his head and swung it at the ball. The golf club whizzed through the air, striking the ball. The ball struck Myron in his top row of teeth, loosening his fronts. Blood filled his grill, and dripped off of his bottom lip. Grunting, God sent golf balls back to back at Myron, breaking different bones in his face and eye socket.

"Aaahhhhhhh! Fuck! Please, stop! Stop, stop it!" Myron begged like a little bitch, tears dripping from his eyes. He had light green snot bubbling out of his left and right nostril, then rolling over his top lip.

"Fuck a stop, bitch!" God screamed at him, with spit flying from his lips. He continued to launch golf balls at Myron's face, breaking more bones and bruising him bluish black. It wasn't long before the nigga's face had blood pouring from out of every cut and crevasse.

*Thock, thock, thock, thock, thock!*

The golf balls looked like white blurs flying through the air and striking Myron in his bloody face, causing him to swell further. Having launched all of the balls at Myron, God's face was shiny from perspiration. Breathing huskily, he wiped the sweat away that threatened to drip from the corner of his brow. He then took stock of the damage he'd caused to Myron. He was fucked up bad. Myron was hanging there with his head bowed, dripping blood from his chin, and the blood splashed on the floor.

"I'm not done witcho bitch-ass yet!" God spat on him and grasped his golf club with both hands, throwing it with all of his might at Myron. The golf club spun around in circles until it struck his chest fast and hard, breaking something in it. Myron howled in pain, as his chest began to turn bluish black from its bruising.

God reached around his back and pulled out a hunting knife from where it was sheathed. He held the shiny metal blade before his eyes, looking at his reflection. He was a stocky brown-skinned dude with a head of naturally curly hair, and a five o'clock shadow lined to perfection. Charity, his daughter's name, was tattooed on the right side of his neck. God took his time admiring the craftsmanship of the hunting knife. After pulling off his black leather glove, he licked his thumb and pressed it against the tip of the blade. Instantly, blood oozed out of his thumb and formed a red dot. God sucked the blood off his thumb and looked at Myron, smiling devilishly. As Myron hollered for help, as loud as he could, over and over again, he slid his leather glove back over his hand. God approached Myron while holding his finger to his lips, shushing him. Terrified, Myron swallowed the lump in his throat and looked at him confusingly. By the look on God's face, he looked like he'd gone completely insane.

God looked at the thick juicy vein on Myron's neck and the twitching of his left pec. He could tell his heart was beating fast and pumping blood rapidly throughout his body. This made him smile harder, thinking of how things were about to get really bloody and gory. Myron's eyes jumped back and forth between God's face and the hunting knife in his hand.

"What the fuck? What the fuck are you about to—" Myron was cut short, as God grasped him by his neck and squeezed hard. His face turned red, and veins bulged all over his face. He winced and gagged, struggling to breathe. God placed the side of his face against Myron's hairy chest, and listened closely to his beating heart. Looking at the left side of his chest, he carved a small X where he planned to begin the first incision of the surgery. Myron bucked and struggled against his grip, as he realized what was about to happen.

God looked into his face, reciting a verse from the Holy Bible. "Romans, chapter twelve, verse nineteen—*Dear friends, never take revenge. Leave that to the righteous anger of God: for the Scriptures say, I will take revenge; I will pay them back, says the Lord.*" Snarling, God slammed his hunting knife through the small X he'd carved into Myron's chest, and dotted his face with blood. Myron's eyes widened, and his mouth stretched open. Scowling, God looked him straight in his eyes and started carving a circle into his left pec, spilling blood everywhere. Once God had completed carving the circle into Myron's chest, he yanked out his knife and switched hands with it. With a few tugs, he opened the hole wide in Myron's chest, and stuck his hand inside of it. He grasped his heart, and pulled it out of his chest, ripping it loose from its valves. Thick blood and goop splattered onto the floor, some of which got on his shoe. God looked at Myron's wet, teary face. His eyes were completely white, and his mouth was hanging open. He was dead!

God's Angels were standing around in the shadows, looking at him like he was crazy. They'd never seen him present this level of savagery before; however, due to the circumstances, they understood where his bloodlust was coming from. God looked to Myron's heart, which was sporadically twitching with each beat it took. He watched it for a while, before driving his hunting knife through it and halting its beating. Yanking his knife back out of it, he dropped the severed heart to the floor and stomped it three times. Afterwards, he dropped his blood knife beside it, and motioned for his angels to follow him out of the basement.

\*\*\*

Charity, a four-year-old little girl, sat on the couch with her Bratz doll, watching cartoons. She had a caramel complexion and hair that looked like it was spun out of gold. At the moment, all of her attention was focused on the television's screen. Nothing—or no one—in the world mattered to her when the Teletubbies were on. Charity was so focused on the flat screen that she didn't pay any attention to Ms. Jones, who was currently inside the kitchen, hunched over the stove. Ms. Jones was a scraggily-looking black woman that had heard it all, seen it all, and had done it all. Coincidently, she was a crackhead, a well-functioning one; but, still a crackhead—no doubt. That didn't stop God from leaving his baby girl with her though. You see, the neighborhood dope man trusted her with his most prized possession, which was his daughter. He'd known the old lady since he was a young man. She'd taught him the game, and was his first customer. They had a solid bond. That couldn't be broken.

Ms. Jones' height was an unimpressive five-foot-two. She was brown-skinned, with a sprinkle of moles on both of her cheeks. The wrinkles around her eyes and neck told the age she was, but she didn't make sixty-six look bad. Especially when considering the fact that she moved around like a twenty-one-year-old woman. At the moment, Ms. Jones was wearing a Santa Claus hat and a plaid shirt. Christmas music played softly from the small old radio sitting on the deep freezer as she busied herself over the stove, whipping soft white cocaine into crack, with black latex gloves on her hands. A Newport cigarette dangled from the corner of her mouth, and her eyelids were narrowed into slits, trying to keep the smoke that rose from the square from out of her eyes. She held one end of the Pyrex pot with one hand, while she used the other hand to whip its contents with a silver spoon. Stopping for a moment, Ms. Jones peered over inside the clear pot to see what she had on her hands.

"This shit needs a little more soda on it," Ms. Jones said. She then walked over to the kitchen table, where there was a box of Arm & Hammer baking soda. She grabbed the box, and noted how light it was. That's when she shook it and peered inside of it, noticing it was indeed empty. Ms. Jones chucked the empty box inside the trash can and walked over to the cabinet. She pulled it opened, and searched for another box of baking soda. Finding it, she switched hands with the cigarette and took the box down. She headed back over to the stove, opening the box. She poured some of its contents into the Pyrex pot, as she stirred up what was inside the murky water. Ms. Jones dumped the ashes from her cigarette into an ashtray, and continued to handle the task at hand. With a smile spread across her thin lips, seeing the cocaine at the bottom of the pot starting to thicken and harden, she said: "Yeahhh, there it is. It's starting to get just right. Just how Momma Jones likes it."

"Charrrrity!" Ms. Jones called out into the living room, as she continued to whip up the crack.

"Yes, Momma Jones?" Charity called out from where she was sitting.

"You hungry in there, mama girl?"

"No, ma'am, I'm fine."

"Okay. Well, you lemme know when you get hungry and I'll whip you up something to eat."

"Yes, ma'am."

"Dashing through the snow in a one-horse open sleigh— over the fields we go, laughing all the way—" Ms. Jones sang along with the Christmas music playing from the radio. She was really feeling the holiday spirit, especially since

God was gonna bless her with twice the amount of crack he did, for whipping up his crack. You see, Ms. Jones was the best whipper in the hood. The old bitch had a wrist game that was blessed by the heavens, and a recipe that was sure to get any fiend hooked. This was the reason why God had hired her to work for him exclusively. He didn't want her working for anyone else, for as long as he had her under him.

Ms. Jones had shown God countless times how to whip the cocaine into crack like she did, and had even given him her recipe, but he refused to do the shit himself. The way he saw it, he was a boss—not a worker—so it didn't make sense for him to cook up his own shit. Nah, it made more sense to pay some mothafuckaz to do it for him. The last thing Ms. Jones was gone do was, complain about having to cook up the young dope man's shit. She's wasn't anyone's fool. She wasn't about to talk herself out of making some money. The way she saw it, for as long as he was paying her, she'd be the one whipping up his shit.

"Momma Jones—" Charity appeared in the doorway of the kitchen, stealing Ms. Jones' attention from the Pyrex pot.

"Yes, mama girl?" Ms. Jones replied, going back to the pot.

"Do you have a paper and ink pen, so I can write down what I want for Christmas?"

Ms. Jones took the cigarette out of her mouth, dumped some ashes, and then looked at Charity. "Yeah, I'll be in there with it once I finish this."

Charity's face frowned, and she looked at the pot that Ms. Jones was mixing something in. "What're you making?"

The question took Ms. Jones off guard. She found herself struggling to come up with an answer. "It's an, uh, um, it's an, uhhhh, it's a cake. Yeah, it's a cake that I'm making."

"What kinda cake, Momma Jones?" she asked curiously.

"A white cake, sweetheart."

"Can I have some of the frosting?"

"Ummm, I'm sorry, mama girl, but this a special kinda cake. This cake I'm making is only for adults. I've got some chocolate brownies in the cupboard if you'd like one, how about that?"

"Yes!" Charity smiled and clapped her hands excitedly. She then got a chocolate brownie out of the cupboard, and began eating it. In doing so, she left chocolate residue all over her mouth. It didn't stop her from eating the delicious treat, though. She loved it. "This is delicious. Thank you, Momma Jones."

"You're welcome, baby girl."

Once Charity went back inside the living room, Ms. Jones finished up her business with the Pyrex pot. She recovered a piece of paper and an ink pen, and gave them to Charity. When Charity started writing down what she wanted for Christmas on the piece of paper, Ms. Jones headed back inside the kitchen to get some paper towels to wipe the chocolate off her mouth. While she was gone, there was knocking at the front door. Charity started to spring up to answer it, but recalled Ms. Jones and her father had warned her not to ever answer the door.

"Who is it?" Ms. Jones called out from the kitchen.

"It's me, Momma Jones!" the voice responded.

"Oh, it's my daddy, Momma Jones!" Charity sprung up from where she was lying writing her list.

"It's me? Boyyy, black folks refuse to say who they are when they show up at your house," Ms. Jones said, as she wiped the chocolate from Charity's mouth and hands. She then balled up the paper towel and headed for the front door, unlocking it. Ms. Jones pulled open the door and stepped aside, allowing God in over the threshold. As soon as the dope man crossed the threshold, Charity smiled and ran over to him. He scooped her in his arms and spun her around. Bringing her back in close to him, he kissed her on the cheek and held her in his arms.

"Hey, daddy," Charity greeted her father.

"Hey, lil' mama, how you been? You ain't been giving Momma Jones a hard time, have you?" God asked.

"Nah, she's been good. I put those cartoons on, and she's been as quiet as a mouse ever since," Ms. Jones said, having just finished closing and locking the door behind her.

"Good. That's what I like to hear. Gemme some." He held out his fist and Charity dapped him up.

"Eskimo kiss, daddy." She brushed her nose against her father's nose. "Now a real kiss." She pecked him on the lips.

"What chu got there?" God took the piece of paper from his daughter, and began looking it over.

"It's my Christmas list, daddy. I started putting everything down that I wanted Santa to bring me, but I haven't finished yet." She looked over the list beside her father.

God had a smirk on his lips as he read over the list. The list was comprised of all of the stuff that your average six-year-old girl would want for Christmas. There was one thing on the list that totally took God by surprise, though. When he saw it, his eyes widened and his mouth hung open. At the center of the list, Charity listed, *I want my mommy to come back from Heaven to visit me.* Instantly, God's eyes began to water, and he found his heart aching all over again, like the day it did when Angela was murdered.

"Is something wrong, daddy?" Charity asked her father.

"Are you all right, God?" Ms. Jones asked him.

God sat Charity down and handed her back her Christmas list. He blinked back tears, and told Ms. Jones,

"I'm straight, Momma Jones. I'll be right back. I've gotta use the bathroom."

God hurried off to the bathroom and slammed the door shut behind him. He then placed his back up against the door, and tilted his head back. His eyes turned glassy and pink. Before he knew it, tears were sliding down his face. Reaching inside his back pocket, he pulled out the picture of his wife, Angela, that he always carried around with him. Angela was a beautiful chocolate woman, with short hair that she wore feathered out at its ends. She had almond shaped eyes, the perfect button nose, and succulent full lips. Her top lip was pink, while the bottom one was a shade lighter than her complexion.

"Damn, bae," God walked over to the medicine cabinet mirror, observing the wallet-sized picture. "Just damn!" He slammed his fist down on the porcelain sink, causing it to vibrate from the impact. Big teardrops fell from his eyes and splashed on the picture, rolling off the end of it. "I shoulda left the streets alone while I was up. I didn't have to beef with the Ortega Brothers. I coulda just let 'em have this shit. I was leaving the game after I finished off my shipment anyway. But, nah, a nigga's pride got in the way and I hadda show 'em just how G I was. And look what the fuck it cost me—"

His eyes became hot with a fresh pair of tears, and his bottom lip trembled. The tears obscured his vision, and then they slid down his cheeks. He sniffled and used the bottom of his shirt to wipe his dripping eyes. "It cost me my beautiful wife, and my daughter her mother. If only I could turn back the hands of time, Angie—If only I could turn back the hands of time, I'd give all of this shit up and leave a square nigga's life. Loading and unloading boxes at UPS and dropping dem shits off." Shutting his eyelids briefly, God took a deep breath, trying to pull himself from his emotional state. When he opened his eyes again, he looked down at the picture of his wife and kissed it. He then slid the picture back into his back pocket, and turned on the faucet. Water rushed from its spout. He cupped his hands underneath the cool, flowing water and splashed it against his face. The water ran down his face in beads, and dripped off of his chin, hitting the porcelain sink.

\*\*\*

*Vroooooom!*

*The engine of a Ducati whined as it sped through the streets, spraying water in its wake, as it flew up the soaked block. Raindrops fell from the murky sky at one hundred miles an hour in the freezing cold. The day was the perfect backdrop for a mothafucka'z death. The driver of the bike was dressed in an all-black helmet and black leather motorcycle suit. His passenger was a nigga dressed identically to him, clutching an Uzi .9mm. He was riding backwards on the bike, with his back up against the rider, scanning the left side of the street for his target, holding his lethal weapon with both gloved hands. The left side of the street showed on the visor of his helmet.*

*The Ducati slowed up as it neared the double doors of a fancy restaurant. A couple had just emerged. They were God and Angela. Angela was holding a folded Los Angeles Times newspaper above her head, letting the falling raindrops pelt against it, shielding her from the wetness as best as it could. While Angela was doing this, her husband, God, was opening up their umbrella.*

*"Hurry up, babe, you'll mess around and catch a cold out here. It's freezing,"* a grinning Angela told her husband

*as she stood hunched down, holding the newspaper above her head. Her face was wet, and her hair was matted against it. Her khaki trench coat was darker on its collar and shoulders from the pouring rain.*

*"I got chu, ma. Gemme a second, this thang jamming up on me," God grinned as he struggled to open the umbrella.*

*"Lemme see, hold this." She handed him the newspaper and took the umbrella. It took a couple of tries, but she finally got the umbrella to open. She held the umbrella up over their heads and said, "There you go. All it needed was a woman's touch." She smiled.*

*"I told you to give up them blocks, mothafucka!" the rider of the Ducati's voice rang out in the cool air.*

*God and Angela's heads whipped around. Their eyes grew big, and their mouths hung open. The reflection of them and the restaurant they came out of was shown on the visor of the gunman's helmet. He pointed his Uzi at the married couple and swept his automatic back and forth.*

*Blatatatatatatatatatat!*

*The horrified screams of God and Angela filled the air as they were cut down by rapid gunfire. They crashed to the sidewalk, the umbrella falling down against the sidewalk right beside them. God lay beside Angela on his stomach, wincing. He had two holes in his back. She lay on her back with several bleeding black holes in her torso. Her eyes were wide open, and her mouth was moving like a fish out of water, blood running out of the corner of her mouth. She stared at God, trying to say something but unable to form the words. Her hands moved towards his hand, trying desperately to hold his hand. Their hands found each other and held tightly.*

*"What—what is it, baby? What—what are you tryna say?" God asked, tears coming out of his eyes from the*

*painful wounds he sustained. At this time, police cars' sirens were wailing, and people were coming outside from the restaurant they were recently at, as well as surrounding businesses, to see what was going on.*

*"I—I love—love you," Angela managed to say, then her mouth trembled. Tears ran out of her eyes, and she blinked her eyelids, trying to fight back the urge to shut them forever.*

*"I love you too, ma. You gotta hang on though. Okay? I can't lose you, we can't lose you, ma. Charity and I need you here with us." He hung on to her hands, feeling her grip loosening. "Oh, my God, Angie, don't leave us. Please, don't leave us, babe. You're my heart, my reason for living. I'd die without you. Baby, I am nothing without you here with me, please, baby, please. Gawd, noooo, no, no, noooo!" God broke down, sobbing and crying like a new born baby, seeing the eyes of his sweetheart become vacant and her movements still.*

*It was right then he knew he'd lost her forever. He scooted over to her, kissed her hand and laid his head against the side of her head. He then shut his eyelids, crying. The raindrops that pelted against his face mixed in with his teardrops, which washed away with the rain. God listened to the police and ambulance sirens. His blood and Angela's mixed in with the pouring rain and dripped off inside the gutter.*

After the shooting, God laid up in the hospital for two months to recover. He then laid low for a year before launching an attack against the Ortega Brothers. On the night he unleashed vengeance, he caught Myron slipping and made him pay dearly. Now the only person he had on his shit list was Myron's older brother, Raheem. Once he exacted his revenge on Raheem, he was sure Angela would be able to rest in peace. Still, the death of one of his wife's murderers didn't do anything to make him feel better. He still felt empty and hurt. It didn't matter, though. He was going to make the last of the Ortega Brothers feel his wrath.

God dried his face on one of the towels hanging on a rack. He then dried his hands, and took one last look into the medicine cabinet mirror to check his appearance. He looked normal enough, so he decided to head out of the bathroom. As soon as he opened the door, Charity jumped out from beside the wall and said 'boo', trying to scare him. Although she didn't honestly scare him, God acted like he was terrified, cowering in the corner inside of the bathroom.

"Daddy, it's just me, silly—your daughter." Charity giggled and ran inside the bathroom, arms open.

"Oh, thank God. I was scared to death. It's just you, baby girl." God scooped Charity into her arms and picked her up, kissing her on the cheek.

"You love yo daddy, lil' mama, huh?" God asked the little girl that held his heart in the palms of her hands.

"Yes. Very, very much." Charity grabbed him by his face and kissed him on the lips.

"Good. 'Cause I love you very, very much also." He looked at something on her chin that had caught his eye. He licked his finger and tried scratching it off. "What's this on yo chin?"

"I'm not sure. Maybe it's chocolate. Momma Jones gave me a chocolate brownie earlier."

"Yeah. That's definitely what it is." He wiped his chocolate-stained finger on his jean leg. When he did this, Charity frowned, seeing something on the tip of her father's sneakers.

"Daddy, is that blood on your shoes?" Charity asked with a frown.

God looked down, and—sure enough—there were speckles of blood on his Jordans. He realized he must have gotten the blood on his sneaker when he cut out Myron's heart. After he'd completed the murder, he dipped off to one of his low-key apartments in the city, where he washed up and changed his clothes. He found it funny that he didn't notice the blood on his sneakers when he went to put the shoes back on. God had decided he'd toss the sneakers into the garbage once he'd gotten home.

"Nah, baby, that's not blood. That's ketchup on daddy's shoe. I was eating hotdogs with some friends of mine today."

"Oh."

God journeyed inside the kitchen, standing in the doorway, watching Momma Jones over the stove.

"You almost done in here?" God asked her.

"Yeah. You wanna gemme a few mo' minutes?"

"No rush, Momma Jones. I'm not taking that with me. You know lil' mama gon' be with me. I'ma have one of my boyz come and get that. They can take it back to the spot."

"Oh, okay."

"Yeah, just take yo cut off the top and put the rest up."

"I got cha."

"Thanks for watching my lil' mama for me." He switched arms with Charity, and reached inside his pocket, pulling out a fat ass wad of blue faces. He peeled off two one-hundred-dollar bills and tried to pass them to Momma Jones, but she didn't accept them.

"Boy, if you don't stop insulting me like that—" Momma Jones popped God's hand and told him to put away his money. "You know good and goddamn well I'm not finna let chu pay me for watching this pretty lil' girl." Momma Jones and Charity smiled at each other, as she caressed the side of her cheek. "It was all my pleasure. As a matter of fact, any time you needa break, you gemme a call, how about that?"

"Alright, I'm not gonna argue with that." He stuffed the money back inside his pocket. "Thanks, Momma Jones." He kissed her on the cheek, and then she let them out of the house. Standing in the doorway, Momma Jones watched God strap his daughter into the baby seat, and then secure himself inside the whip he was driving.

# Chapter 5

### *The next day*

After being searched thoroughly by a female corrections officer, Billie was finally able to enter the visiting room. She stopped at the center of the room, and looked everyone over, trying to find her baby daddy, Joaquin. There was a lot of noise in the room, as people were talking to their incarcerated loved ones. The room was sort of crowded, so she couldn't see her daughter's father. It wasn't until he lifted his arm in the air and waved his hand that she spotted him.

A smile spread across Billie's face, and she made her way in Joaquin's direction. She found him sitting at the end of one of the tables. Fully grown, at twenty-six, Joaquin stood six-foot-one and had a slender body defined by muscle. He had a clean-shaven face, and wore his long curly hair in four cornrows. When he spotted Billie, he cracked a one-sided grin and rose to his feet. He greeted her with a quick hug and a kiss on the cheek. They then sat down across from one another.

Billie frowned as she examined Joaquin's eyes and movements. He had all of the classic symptoms of a person that was high: dilated pupils, runny nose, and shakiness. Although Joaquin wasn't shaking like that, she could tell something was up with him. She seriously wished he wasn't still using, because he'd promised her—when he'd gotten locked up—that he was going to stop.

"Joaquin, are you high?" Billie asked, concerned.

Joaquin looked at her like that was a stupid ass question to ask him. He sniffled and rubbed his nose, saying, "Hell no! What the fuck make you ask me something like that? I told you I was done with that shit after what happened that night."

"Ummm, huh—" She narrowed her eyelids at him suspiciously. "Lemme find out, and I'ma kick yo black ass." Joaquin chuckled. "I'm not playing witchu, nigga."

"Anyway," Joaquin waved her off and changed the subject, "how're you doing out there?" He threw his head to the right, referring to the outside world. When he said this, Billie looked down for a second, then back up at him. His forehead creased because he knew what that meant. Something was wrong.

"I got fired," she said sadly.

"For real? What happened?" he asked, concerned.

Billie filled Joaquin in on what had happened on the day she was fired.

"Damn!" Joaquin shook his head and ran his hand down his face. He knew that if she had been fired, she was going to have a hard time taking care of their daughter and keeping money on his books. His books he wasn't too worried about, but his daughter was an entirely different thing all together. Nothing—and no one—in this world was more important than Annabelle to him. He'd kill for her and die for her. No *ifs, ands* or *buts* about it. "Shit tight, huh?"

"Yeah," Billie nodded. She knew he was referring to her finances being tight. "You know unc tried to help me out, but I wasn't having that. If that helping hand ain't coming from you, I don't want it. You know how we do."

"I understand." Joaquin nodded.

"Look, I don't want chu worrying about us out there. I got us faded." She looked him square in the eye, then added with a serious tone: "I'ma 'bouta lay down a play that'll take care of you and lil' mama."

Billie and Joaquin had met six years ago at a hole-in-the-wall spot called *The Bar Fly*. She was hustling men that believed because she was a woman, she didn't know a thing about shooting pool. Billie played twenty games of pool that night and won everyone. She had so much money she was running out of places to put it. Unbeknownst to her, Joaquin had been watching her from his table within the shadows. He liked how she carried herself, so he decided to make his move. The first thing Billie noticed when he introduced himself was how pleasing he was to her eyes, and his thick Spanish accent. It had caught her off guard. She'd expected him to speak like the rest of the brothers from South Central, Los Angeles. She loved his accent though. It added to his sex appeal.

Joaquin got Billie to agree to a game of pool for the rest of her winnings, which was a little less than ten grand. He upped the stakes a little, though. If he won, not only would he get the money from the bet, he'd also get a kiss. With the particulars of the game disclosed, Billie and Joaquin went on to play. Joaquin was such a great shot that Billie didn't even get a chance to shoot. He pocketed his winnings and offered to buy her a drink. They drank beers and conversed until closing time rolled around. Billie didn't want the night to end, so she invited Joaquin back to her place. One thing led to another, and they winded up sleeping together. That very night, Annabelle was conceived. During her second month of pregnancy, Joaquin popped the question and she said *yes*.

From there on out, their lives seemed to be the things fairy tales were made of. Well, that was until Joaquin started fucking around on her. He was nailing everything with a pulse, and he wasn't showing any signs of stopping. Billie would always take him back. It wasn't just because she loved him; she wanted to give her daughter what she didn't have growing up—a family! When they'd gotten back together again, things had been going beautifully between them for quite some time. But Joaquin, *being* Joaquin, had to go and fuck things up. His whorish ways not only ended their relationship, it landed him in the situation he was in now.

\*\*\*

*Joaquin and Billie were both drunk and high, dancing out on the floor. Billie was bent over, grinding her big old ass into his crotch while holding onto the ends of his blazer. The disco balls spinning from the ceiling cast the violet color on them. The couple didn't pay the spectacular light show any mind as they continued with their sexualized dancing. Suddenly, Billie came up and grabbed Joaquin by his tie, pulling him closer. She turned her head over her shoulder, closed her eyelids, and kissed him slow and sensually. Their lip locking drove Joaquin crazy, and had his dick as hard as a kilo of coke. He loved when his lady sex-played him. That shit really turned him on, and made him eager to give her some of that thug passion.*

*Billie released Joaquin's tie and bent over, touching the floor. He placed one hand on her ass, while the other held onto his golden bottle of Ace of Spades. His eyes were focused solely on her ass as she bumped and ground against him. Joaquin's eyes wandered up from Billie's bodacious bottom and he locked eyes with a young lady sitting at the bar. She was a fair-skinned beauty with curly, sandy brown hair, slanted eyes, high cheek bones, and full lips, courtesy of her Nigerian heritage. She was in a black and gold dress that hugged her curvy form and boasted all of her most prized attributes. Shorty had been chit-chatting with her girls while keeping an eye on Joaquin since he'd entered the club, taking casual sips of her daiquiri. Joaquin could tell, by the way she'd been eying him, that she wanted a taste of what he had. Truth be told, he wanted a piece of what she had to offer too. The only thing holding him up was the presence of Billie, and the vow he made to never to break her heart again, for the one hundredth millionth time.*

*Old girl, keeping her eyes on Joaquin, sat her drink down on the bar top and said something to her girls. She nodded toward the hallway where the women's rest room was located, and Joaquin nodded his understanding. With the exchange made, shorty pulled her rising dress back down her thighs and sashayed her way toward the hallway. She threw her ample ass from side to side, and glanced over her shoulder, making sure Joaquin was watching her. Seeing that she had his attention, he smiled and she batted her eyelashes, seductively.*

*"Baby, hold this, I'll be right back," Joaquin told Billie, as he passed her his bottle of Ace of Spade.*

*"Where you going, bae?" Billie asked, clutching the expensive golden bottle.*

*"Shit, I gotta drain the main vein; that champagne has finally got to me," he said, grabbing hold of the bulge in his slacks, watching his lady turn the bottle up. He took the bottle from her and took it to the head, spilling some of it down his chin. Bringing the bottle down, he wiped his dripping chin and passed the bottle back to Billie. She switched hands with the bottle and pulled him close, kissing him.*

*"Hurry up, so we can get outta here, alright? I want some of my dick!" Billie grabbed his bulge, and he grunted. Joaquin cracked a smirk and smacked Billie on her ass, heading for the women's rest room. En route to the hallway, he slipped a vial of cocaine from out of his pocket and*

*tapped it above his fist. A small mountain of coke manifested on his hand and he snorted it, licking the residue that was left behind.*

*Joaquin glanced over his shoulder and saw Billie alone on the floor. Her eyelids were shut, and she was moving from side to side, snapping her fingers. Every now and then she'd take a swig from the champagne. A light-skinned dude slowly crept up on her while she was getting her groove on. He was a tall nigga who wore his hair faded on the sides, with a naturally curly top. He was dressed in a copper-brown suit, which left his bare, muscular chest on display. He had an obsessive amount of jewelry decorating his neck, wrists, and fingers. The diamonds in his earlobes were huge and sparkling. Homeboy wore what most women would call a sexy smile, as he bumped up against Billie and started grinding on her. Joaquin's face twisted into a scowl. He rolled up his sleeves and was about to put that pretty mothafucka in his place. He'd taken his first step forward, when he noticed Billie turn around and gently push him off of her. They exchanged some words and the dude backed up, smiling, holding his hands up. Right after, Billie went back to her dancing, and drinking from the bottle of Ace of Spades.*

*Joaquin smiled, seeing his lady handle herself like she was supposed to, but that still didn't stop him from attending his pussy appointment inside the women's rest room. He turned back around and retreated to the rest room, where he'd meet the enticing young woman that had flirted with him earlier. As soon as Joaquin entered the women's rest room, he found the object of his lust smiling. She was leaning up against the door of one of the stalls, with her arms folded across her breasts.*

*"Well, damn, handsome, it took you long enough," the young lady said, as she swept her dangling curls from out of her face. "You got party refreshments?"*

*Smiling, Joaquin pulled out his vial of cocaine and a black flask with a gold crucifix engraved on it. He dangled them both in front of little mama's eyes and said, "Pick your poison."*

*"How about 'em both?" she said, snatching the flask from him and removing its top. She turned the flask up, guzzling it, throat moving up and down her neck. As she wiped her mouth free of the alcohol, she passed the flask back to Joaquin, who was in the middle of snorting coke from off his fist. He guzzled from the flask and slipped it back inside his blazer. He tapped some of the coke out of the vial onto his fist, creating a small pile, and motioned her over to indulge. She pulled her curly hair back into a ponytail and snorted up the small pile. Instantly, she threw her head back and blinked her eyelids. Her eyes were teary, and the tingles she felt in her nostrils tempted her to sneeze. Bringing her head back down, she pulled on her nose and told Joaquin how good his coke was. He snorted up some more and she pulled him into her by his collar, kissing him deep and hard. Afterwards, she shoved open the door of one of the stall, and pulled him inside, slamming the door shut behind him.*

*Little mama didn't waste any time getting Joaquin out of his slacks and sucking his dick. While she was bobbing up and down on his dick, he treated his nasal passages to the nose-candy from his vial. Once he was rock hard, shorty came back up and snorted some coke off of his fist. They kissed some more, and she slipped off her thong, leaving it hanging around one of her ankles. He sat his vial on top of the metal box that contained the extra roll of towel tissue. Shortly thereafter, he lifted homegirl up against the wall and she wrapped her legs around his waist. She held on to the top of the stall's wall. Joaquin assisted in holding her up with one hand, and used the other to guide himself inside of her. She gasped and threw her head back. Her eyes rolled to their whites, feeling him enter warm, slick center. Joaquin started off slow stroking her, making her wetter and wetter. Then, he sped up, going long and deep inside of her, hitting that spot she so desperately needed him to touch. Soon, the stall's wall was banging, rattling noisily, with Joaquin pounding shorty out. Her sexual cries of pleasure resonated throughout the women's rest room, and turned the women entering away.*

*"Girl, can you believe some ho in there getting fucked in the women's rest room? I gotta pee too—Y'all hoes gon' have to huddle around me while I go into one of them empty champagne bottles at the table," a five-foot-two, honey-complexioned chick with a short haircut and pink spandex dress told her group of friends. They'd just left the women's rest room where Joaquin was packing homegirl out.*

*Billie, who was journeying down the hallway, had overheard the girl in the pink spandex dress, and her face scrunched up. She was looking for Joaquin since he'd been gone for quite some time. She'd overheard the girl in the pink dress, and got a weird feeling in the pit of her stomach. Something told her that Joaquin was the one nailing old girl to the cross in the women's rest room. Although she didn't know for sure that it was her man laying the pipe down, the mere thought of it being him brought tears to her eyes. As soon as one dropped from her right eye, she wiped her eye with her curled finger and sniffled. Then she got extremely angry. Her heart thudded as she neared the women's rest room. She pushed the door open, and she could hear the unified sexual grunts of a man and woman. This made her heart thud enough harder, and she started to feel queasy.*

*'Please, God, do not let this be my man! Do not let this be Joaquin, please, Lord,' Billie thought as she approached the stall door that the noise was coming from. Stopping at the stall door, she downed the last of the champagne from the bottle and took a deep breath. Now, that she'd prepared herself for what she would possibly see, she snatched open the stall's door and was devastated at the sight before her. Joaquin had shorty held up against the stall door, fucking her pussy, mercilessly. The devastation disappeared from Billie's face, and she mad-dogged Joaquin.*

*"Nigga, you ain't shit, witcho dog ass!" Billie hollered out, startling them both. They hurriedly started getting dressed. With fire burning in her eyes, Billie set her sights on the ho Joaquin had been fucking. Her face frowned up, and she twisted her lips. "And, bitch, you ain't shit either, you knew this was my man! Unh huh, see I'm 'bouta beat both of y'all asses! Come here, trick!" Billie grabbed old girl by her curly hair, pulling her from out of the stall and tearing the stitching that held the weave to her natural hair. Blood oozed out of the girl's scalp, and she hollered out in excruciation. Holding that bitch by her hair, Billie took the bottle by its neck and started clubbing her ass with it. Broken teeth flew from out of the girl's mouth and her blood dotted the floor. Her eyes were flickering white, and the entire lower half of her face was drenched in blood.*

*Breathing heavily, Billie let the poor girl drop to the floor, and turned around to Joaquin. She slowly approached him with tears streaming down her cheeks, her bottom lip trembling. The man who claimed to have loved her most in the world had crushed her mentally and emotionally. Joaquin felt like shit. He knew Billie was probably about to beat his ass, and he was going to let her. He reasoned that was the least he could do after cheating on her, yet again.*

*Stopping before Joaquin, Billie pulled off her platinum engagement ring and gave it to him. He looked down at the ring in his palm and felt an explosion of reoccurring pain in his balls. He dropped the engagement ring and grabbed himself, eyes bulging. After kicking him in the nuts, Billie followed up by clocking him upside the head with the Ace of Spades bottle. Dizzy, he fell to the floor beside homegirl he was fucking, bleeding from the side of his head and moaning in pain. With the damage done, Billie stared down at her ex-fiancé and the ho he'd been nailing. She sniffled and dropped the bloody golden champagne bottle beside them, making her way out of the women's rest room.*

*Still holding his aching balls, Joaquin crawled over to homegirl whom Billie had bludgeoned, and checked her pulse. She was still alive, but she'd been brutally beaten. Pulling out his cellular, he dialed 9-1-1 and told them someone had beaten his friend. He'd given the dispatcher the club's address, when the girl's friends spilled into the women's rest room. They were visibly shocked when they found her battered and bloody. They fired off a series of questions at Joaquin, which he vaguely answered. He held himself as he limped towards the rest room door. He'd gotten halfway across the floor, when the door flew open and the paramedics rushed in with a gurney. The police weren't far behind, so he hurried up and got the fuck out of there. He didn't fuck with the law, and he wasn't about to answer any of their questions.*

*The DJ had stopped playing the music, and the lights were now on inside the club. Everyone was in the know about the disturbance that had taken place inside the women's rest room. While everyone was heading towards the women's rest room to find out exactly what happened, Joaquin was making his way through the crowd. He called out for Billie and scanned the clubbers for her face. When he didn't see her, he figured she was outside; so he made way for the exit. Joaquin had come out of the club in time to see Billie across the street in the parking lot. She was flirting with homeboy who'd been trying to dance with her earlier. A smile was plastered across their faces, as she appeared to be programming her telephone number into his cell phone. Joaquin frowned up heatedly, seeing what was going down. After looking both ways, he jogged across the street towards Billie and homeboy. He jumped over the chain that separated the parking lot from the sidewalk and approached his lady and his potential replacement.*

*"Yo, my man, she's with me," Joaquin told homeboy who'd just gotten his cellular back from Billie.*

*"First of all," homeboy began. "My name isn't 'man'. It's Antoine, bruh. Second of all, shorty just told me she's single. So, if you feel some kind of way, maybe you should keep yo bitch on a leash, so she'll stop wandering over into other niggaz' yards. You feel me?" He stepped to Joaquin and balled his fists at his sides. His face was fixed with an infuriated expression. He looked like he was ready to beat the dog shit out of Joaquin. He was confident that he could too, since he was a former amateur boxer.*

*Billie was appalled about being called a bitch by the dude. She didn't plan on fucking with him anyway. She was using him to make Joaquin jealous. She wanted him to feel how she felt when she caught him fucking that bitch in the women's rest room. Little mama didn't have a problem with going up Antoine's head, but she knew what she was capable of. She'd fuck around and kill that pretty mothafucka! Hell, for that matter, she knew that Joaquin would too. Her baby daddy wasn't any joke when it came to the hands or the guns. Now, though she knew she should intervene in what would lead up to Antoine's demise, but her Uncle Kershawn always told her to stay out of grown men business.*

*"So, uh, I guess we're 'bouta throw hands now, huh?" Joaquin asked.*

*"I don't know, nigga, you tell me. I mean, you the one fronting like you tryna fight over a bitch!" Antoine said, looking him up and down like he wasn't shit.*

*Joaquin chuckled and pulled his nose, glancing back at Billie. Swiftly, he whipped back around to Antoine, kicking him in the side of his knee and dropping him down to one. Following up, he chopped him in throat causing him to gag and grasp his neck. Down on one knee, Antoine gagged and coughed while his eyes bulged. Right after, he came down on his hands and knees, throwing up the cheap liquor and wings he'd eaten earlier that night.*

*Meanwhile, Joaquin opened the driver's door of his whip, slid on a pair of black leather gloves and grabbed his shit. He screwed a silencer onto the barrel of his gun. By the time Joaquin cocked his banger, the paramedics were rolling out old girl on a gurney, with her friends and some club goers bringing up the rear. Joaquin slammed his door and advanced in Antoine's direction. A hostile look was on his face, and his gun was gripped at his side.*

*Billie's eyes bulged, seeing Joaquin coming back strapped. Her head whipped back and forth between him and Antoine. "Antoine, get in your car and get the fuck outta here! Now!"*

*"Fuck yo punk-ass baby daddy! I'm not scared of 'em!" Antoine said with glassy eyes and a rope of saliva hanging from his bottom lip. He looked in the direction Joaquin was coming from and saw the gun in his hand. His eyes bulged*

114

*and he scrambled to his feet, taking off running toward his car. Antoine had just opened the driver's door of his whip when a sharp pain exploded in his arm. He clenched his jaws and looked at his arm, teary eyed. Blood was running from a hole in his bicep, and his arm was aching terribly. He was confident the bullet that had struck him had fractured his bone. Looking up, Antoine saw Joaquin approaching him, firing his gun continuously. The second bullet entered the grill of his car while the third one shattered the driver side window, broken glass raining down onto the pavement, sparkling.*

*Seeing the action unfolding before their eyes, the cops that had arrived at the club with the paramedics drew their guns, and made hurried footsteps across the busy street. Billie fled the parking lot and flagged down a taxi. Joaquin took off running in the opposite direction. He made his way down an alley, where he'd discovered a green trash bin. He tossed the gun he'd used to pop Antoine into the trash bin. He peeled off his black leather gloves and stuffed them inside of it also. Next, he straightened out his hair and clothes and casually strolled out of the alley. He made a right out of the alleyway and made his way down the sidewalk. He slipped his hands inside of his slacks and acted as naturally as he could. Hearing police car sirens approaching, Joaquin tensed a little but he continued to play it cool. At the corner of his eye, he saw a police car following alongside him. The cop on the passenger side called out for him, and he broke into a run. The police car pursued him, quickly closing the distance. A few minutes later, Joaquin was boxed in by four police cars and forced down on to the sidewalk. Once he was handcuffed, he was placed into the back of a police car and driven away to face his fate.*

\*\*\*

Joaquin looked at her with narrowed eyelids and furrowed brows. "What chu talking about?"

"I think you already know what I'm talking about." She gave him a knowing look. It was from this look that Joaquin knew that she was talking about getting back in the murder game.

"You know you gave that life up once I touched down in here, just so that there wouldn't be a chance of lil' mama being out there alone, right? If something was to happen to you, then what?"

"Risks were made to be taken. Besides—should shit go left, then Kershawn will take care of her."

"Then she'll end up like us, ma. Cold-blooded killaz. I'm sure neither of us would want that, right?"

"That's not gonna happen. My uncle wouldn't do that. As a matter of fact, I'ma make sure he knows that *that* is not to happen under any circumstances."

"Look, my bad if I came at chu the wrong way, but I just want what's best for our daughter. And as you know, neither of our lives is ideal for her."

"I know that, Joaquin. I'm sure unc knows that too."

Joaquin looked down and nodded understandingly. Looking back up into Billie's eyes, he took her hands into his and rubbed them with his thumbs. A grin etched at the corner of his lips and she blushed, looking away. She hated herself at that moment. She didn't know what it was about him, but his look and his touch always seemed to make her melt like butter. She was sure he knew it too, which was why he always used her love for him against her.

"So, uh, have you given some thought about us getting back together?" Joaquin asked, narrowing his eyelids into slits and biting down on his bottom lip. He was giving her that sexy ass expression that he knew made her putty in his hands. Though Billie was a straight-up killa, she was still a woman with feelings and emotions like any other female. Wanting to feel loved, safe, protected, and provided for was coded into her DNA. It was a part of her nature. It was something that she couldn't help. Joaquin understood that fully. And that's why he'd always been a ladies' man.

"Of course I have," Billie said, as she batted her eyelashes and smiled. She felt so giddy in his presence. Even when she was hot at him, he always managed to somehow break through her tough exterior. She'd been working on combating her emotions though. She knew that he wasn't any good for her. Joaquin would never change his ways for her. No matter how much he claimed to love her and their daughter. It was something she believed he loved just a little bit more. What that was, you ask? Pussy!

"And?" Joaquin asked smirking, tilting his head aside.

Billie, looking serious, cleared her throat and took a deep breath. She looked into Joaquin eyes and said, "And then, I remember all the pain and heartache you put me through, Joaquin." She pulled her hands away from him. He looked at her with a furrowed brow. He was confused. He thought she was going to fall for his advances again, but she'd surprised him. "What you done to me hurt—" Billie became teary eyed, and her voice cracked emotionally. "It hurt me to the core of my soul." A teardrop fell from her right eye, and she used her curled finger to wipe away the wetness. Joaquin stared at her, feeling like a piece of shit.

"Baby, look, I'm s—" Joaquin began, but Billie cut him short.

"*I'm sorry, I'm sorry, I'm sorry,*" Billie mocked him, tilting her head from side to side. "Don't chu get tired of this

Tranay Adams

same song and dance between us, Joaquin? We've been doing this shit for years now, and frankly, I'm tired of it. You think Annabelle doesn't see how you've been hurting me? You're not afraid that she's gonna grow up and think that your kind of behavior is acceptable from the man claiming to love her?" She frowned and looked at him. "Tell me, how would you feel if a man treated Annabelle like you treated me?" she asked.

Joaquin frowned angrily, and his nostrils flared. "I'd kill that mothafucka."

"Right," Billie nodded. She took a deep breath, obviously tired of his bullshit. "Look, I've gotta go. Try to call the house later today so Annabelle can talk to you. She loves and misses you."

Hearing his baby girl loved and missed him made him smile. "Oh, yeah? Tell my lil' mama daddy loves and misses her, too."

"I'll be sure to relay the message," Billie told him, dabbing her wet eyes with a Kleenex. Once she'd dried her eyes, she rose from the table and turned to leave.

"Well, damn, so I don't getta hug and '*I love you*' or nothing before you bounce up outta here?" Joaquin asked with a wrinkled forehead and smirk.

Billie hesitantly hugged him and told him she loved him. He tried to kiss her on the lips, but she turned her head. His lips landed on her cheek.

"I gotta go, Joaquin," Billie told him. She turned around and walked away. Joaquin stood watching her sashay across the visiting room floor.

"Don't worry, ma, I'ma make things right! I promise," Joaquin called out to her before she disappeared from the visiting room.

118

\*\*\*

After he came back from his visit, Joaquin made his way to the assignment he was given inside the laundry room, walking past several inmates who were hard at work on the job they were given. Unbeknownst to him, he'd just walked past Frog, a man that would play a significant role in his life in the near future. At the time, Frog was separating the laundry so it could be washed.

Some of the laundry had shit and piss stains in them that Frog knew wasn't going to come clean, no matter how many times he washed them. But he didn't give a fuck. He was only there to do the task that was assigned to him. And that's it. He didn't give a shit if the laundry came clean, because he wasn't going to be the poor bastard wearing the shit. Nah, you see, he had enough dough on his books to buy fresh socks, draws, undershirts and everything else he needed while he was on lock.

While Frog busied himself separating the clothing, he had a hushed conversation with a corrections officer, who had his arms folded across his chest, pretending to be looking over all of the convicts in the working facility. Frog was a rotund Mexican man with bubble eyes, an under bite and a double chin that gave him a frog-like appearance. Frog was a dangerous man who preferred to handle his issues with a knife, as opposed to a gun.

"You know that guy you were telling me about on the outside—that sends mothafuckaz on permanent vacations?" Frog asked the corrections officer, known in the corrections facility as Officer Murtaugh. Murtaugh was a tall, white dude that any race of women would consider attractive, especially with his muscular build. He was a hard-ass who never appeared to be happy, unless he was going to benefit from it. Within the walls, he had a reputation for being a barbarian, having brutalized disrespectful inmates and whipped a couple of his co-workers' asses. With knowledge of how the Irish-American bad boy got down, Murtaugh's peers and the facility's inmates stayed the fuck out of his way. And that's exactly the way he liked it!

"Yeah, what about 'em?" Murtaugh asked, not even looking at him. He wanted to give the impression that he wasn't paying any mind to Frog. He wanted it to look like he was just minding his business and keeping his eyes on the inmates while they did their day-to-day jobs.

"I want this mayate that killed my brother tightened up."

The *mayate* Frog was referring to was God. He'd gotten word not long ago that he was the one that had tortured and killed his brother, Myron. Right now he was willing to pay whatever to have the dope man's head knocked off his shoulders.

"It's gonna cost ya."

"No shit. Ain't shit in this life free, what we talking?"

"I don't know. I'll have to check with my guy. But chu will kick seven thousand, five hundred dollars up front to me for making the contact. That's non-refundable. Meaning, if you decide not to go through with extracting whomever this fuck is, I still get paid."

"Oh, you don't have to worry about me pulling out on the arrangement. I can fade whatever the cost is. Believe that."

"Alright. I'm gonna need a name and a picture."

Once Murtaugh said this, Frog looked around to make sure no one was spying on him, before pulling out a wallet-sized picture and handing it to the crooked corrections officer. Murtaugh studied the picture. He then turned the picture over, and saw the government name of the man on the picture, as well as his street name—which was *God*.

"Alright. We've got something we can work with here. I'll get in touch witchu tomorrow." Murtaugh tucked the picture inside his breast pocket and walked off to check on the other inmates working inside the laundry room.

\*\*\*

### *The next day*

Frog was busy separating the dirty undergarments when he was approached by corrections officer Murtaugh again. The crooked officer stopped in the center of the aisle, and pretended to be tying up his pattern leather boot, while talking to Frog.

"I talked to my guy. He says fifty gees will get that situation of yours taken care of for you. With my fifteen percent finder's fee, you're looking at fifty-seven thousand, five hundred dollars. You can manage that, right?" Murtaugh asked him.

"Yeah. I suspected I was gonna hear from you today. I'ma leave you with the card to contact my lady out there. She'll make sure you get the bag." Frog finished sorting out the garments. He then walked over to the end of the big gray bin on wheels, and pulled it along behind him. He dropped a card beside Murtaugh, as he passed him so casually that no one even noticed it.

Murtaugh picked up the card and tucked it inside his breast pocket. He then walked back up the aisle, whistling and looking around at all the inmates as they performed the tasks they were given.

### *Later that day*

"I got cho next big thing," Kershawn announced to Billie, pulling a wallet-sized picture of God out of his suit and passing it to Billie. She'd just plopped down beside him on the couch. "Kyree 'God' Purdy."

"Damn, this nigga fine as a mothafucka! Hey, Zaddy," Billie smiled and licked her lips at the picture.

"Yeah, well, his fine ass is worth fifty gees dead."

"Fifty?" Her forehead wrinkled.

"Yep. I went up since you've been gon'. With all of these surveillance cameras and snitches around, shiiiiit, murder isn't an easy task nowadays. Yo ass get caught up, you gon' need that money for an attorney to fight on your behalf. You feel what I'm saying?"

"Most def', unc." She focused her attention back on the picture.

"Already did some of the homework for you. On the back of that picture I scribbled a few places that he frequents." He pointed to the picture, motioning her to turn it over. "Gon' turn it over."

Billie turned the picture over and looked at the list of places that Kershawn had written down. There were bars, strip clubs, casinos, etc. "Alright. Now we got something I can work with."

"I'd pay special close attention to The Pussy Kat Club. My sources told me he spends a lot of time there."

"Pussy Kat Club, huh? That place is still open after all of these years? Well, I know where my next job is gonna be." Billie cracked a smile as she stared down at the picture.

# Chapter 6

### *That night*

A black on black Lamborghini truck pulled up outside The Pussy Kat Club—an exotic strip club. The sports utility vehicle was followed by luxury car after luxury car, lining up one after the other. The driver's door of the Lamborghini opened up, and a young nigga rocking a gold chain with a medallion the size of a saucer, hopped out. He adjusted his baseball cap and walked over to the opposite side of the truck. He opened the front passenger door and stood aside, allowing the passenger to un-board. God stepped out of the Lamborghini truck, taking in the scenery, and rubbing his hands together in anticipation. It had been a while since he'd been out to enjoy himself. So he was looking forward to seeing the big booty strippers The Pussy Kat Club was known to have working the poles. God was dripping heavily in a black Givenchy cap, matching sweatshirt and sneakers. He accessorized with an icy gold bust of his baby girl, Charity, and a bust-down Rolex.

God and his angels mobbed up to the door of The Pussy Kat Club, thick as a mothafucka. Stopping before the gentleman at the door, who was wearing a black turtle neck and blazer, God pulled out a big ass knot of dead presidents and counted off six bills, passing them to the dude at the door. He then pulled off another one hundred dollar bill, and tucked it into the pocket of the doorman's blazer. That one hundred dollar bill was his tip.

"We good?" God asked him.

"Aye, one, big dawg," the doorman said, dapping him up.

God patted him on the shoulder and made his way through the entrance of the gentlemen's club, without getting patted down. You see, God was known up in that piece; so he was given a wide berth. He spent a lot of money up in there, so he was able to move around in the booty club like he owned that mothafucka.

As soon as God and his goons crossed the threshold inside the establishment, they were bombarded by loud music and spinning disco balls. There were half naked women walking back and forth across them. They were either asking the men in the place if they wanted a lap dance, or serving them food and/or alcohol beverage of their choosing. God found the tables that he and his niggaz would take up for the night. He then ordered up bottles of the club's most expensive champagne and hot wings. Although he didn't fuck with the food they served at the strip club, he knew most of his niggaz did. It wasn't that the food they served there was bad. Nah, it wasn't that. It was something about eating food at the same place that women were shaking their ass and pussy that didn't quite sit right with him.

Once the bottles were accounted for at the tables for him and his goons, God grabbed one and popped the lid on it. Foam rose out of the mouth of the bottle and ran over his knuckles. He quickly took it to the head, guzzling the shit like it was water. Bringing the bottle back down from his mouth, he wiped his chin with the back of his jeweled hand, taking a gander around the club at the women he thought he may want to entertain that night.

Seeing that there were plenty of fine ass women in attendance that he didn't mind breaking bread with, God ordered up ten thousand dollars in singles and a money gun.

Once he loaded the gun up, he took the liberty to spark up a fat ass blunt, puffing on the end of it.

"Alright, y'all, we gotta new booty on duty! So, please break out cha wallets and give a warm welcome to the stunning, the amazing, the spectacular—*Snake Eyez!*" DJ Flip introduced Billie by her stage name. A moment later, the lights went out in the club, and left all of the exotic dancers in the establishment in glowing, skimpy clothing. The ladies' hair, pupils, lips, nails, bikini tops and bottoms, as well as the glitter on them, were glowing in neon colors, green, blue, yellow, pink, etc.

*Boom! Boom! Boom! Boom!*
*Frooosh! Frooosh! Frooosh! Frooosh!*

Big flames erupted at the four corners of the stage and licked the air, startling the men sitting at some of the nearby tables. Right after, a spotlight shone on the curtains, and Monifah's *Touch It* dropped.

*Jack Knight and Dakoda House*
*All we wanna do is make you bounce*
*Monifah, would you turn me out?*
*Show me what your thing is all about*

A second later, Billie's fine ass stepped out in her costume. She was wearing a white, banged wig that hung down to her stomach, and yellow cat eye lenses. The black leather corset she wore enhanced her succulent breasts and ass. She had on long black velvet gloves that nearly reached her armpit, and black leather hooker boots that reached her thick thighs. She twirled around a black leather whip, and danced around on the stage provocatively, keeping all of the men's attention. They lusted after her as they threw twenties, fifties and one hundred dollar bills, all of which came raining down upon the stage, like raindrops.

*Do you really wanna touch it*
*Do you really wanna mess with me tonight*
*Oh, and if you know how I like it*
*Would you call my name and give it to me right*
The entire time she was performing, she kept her eyes on God, and he kept his eyes on her. He continuously smoked his blunt. Smoke wafted around him as he shot Benjamin Franklins at her through the money gun.
*Frick, frick, frick, frick, frick!*
The dead presidents shot out of the money gun rapidly, coating the stage with United States' currency. Billie hung her leather whip around her neck, and danced in the falling dollars like it was rain. Keeping his eyes on her, God switched hands with the blunt he was smoking and reloaded the gun with fresh, crispy one hundred dollar bills. While he was doing this, Billie took her whip from around her neck and thrashed it to its full length. She then threw it at the table of a geeky-looking white dude. The end of the whip wrapped around a Corona bottle, and Billie pulled it forward. She caught the bottle in her free hand, and it splashed upon impact. She then turned the bottle completely up, keeping her eyes on God and guzzling it.

God watched as bubbles filled the bottle, as it contents splashed down Billie's throat. Billie spat all over the Corona bottle, then lathered it up with her saliva, stroking it up and down like it was a dick. She did a split on stage, stuck the bottle inside of her mouth down to its neck and pressed her finger at the bottom of it. Slowly, she began to push down on its bottom and work her mouth like a snake would its jaws. The more she did this, the more the Corona bottle slid down her throat. 'Ooohs' and 'Awws' spread throughout the audience of perverted men, as they looked on, eyes big and mouths open.

"That's my new favorite bitch up here!" one man said.

"I'd marry that hoe right now for that shit she doing, dawg!" another man said.

"I think I'm in love!" a different man said, looked toward his homeboy who sitting beside him.

Billie continued to push down the bottle until it had disappeared completely inside of her mouth. When she did this shit, niggaz threw more dollars out on the stage. Their dicks were hard, and they were ready to pay whatever she wanted so they could take her home with them.

Billie placed her lips to the stage. Her throat moved up and down, and little by little her mouth moved up from off the surface. The Corona bottle oozed out of her mouth, slippery with her spit. The more Billie's head moved up from the floor, the more of the Corona bottle was revealed, until it was in full view for everyone to see. Breathing heavily, breasts rising and falling, Billie picked up the Corona bottle. She looked around at all of the men in attendance, showing off the beer bottle. Right then, she slid back up on her feet and gave the bottle to a man holding out handful of twenty dollar bills for his purchase of it. She gladly took his money, folded it and stuffed it between her tits, while the thirsty man held on to the Corona bottle like it was a souvenir.

"I love you, Snake Eyez!" a man called out from the audience, with his hands cupped around his mouth. Billie whipped around to him, kissed her palm and blew him a kiss. He caught the imaginary kiss and fell back in his chair, fainting. Yeah, for real! The nigga really fainted.

Billie motioned for another man to rise from his chair. Once he did, she used her whip to grab one of the legs of the chair, and pulled it into her. The chair went up in the air and she caught it, placing it down on the center of the stage. Billie looked to God, motioned him over and patted the seat of the chair. God couldn't believe she was calling him upon the stage. He wanted to be sure before he went up.

"Me? You sure?" God asked, eyebrows raised and pointing his thumb at his chest. Billie smiled sexily at him, and coiled and uncoiled her finger at him, invitingly.

Excited, God handed one of his angels the money gun, and mashed his blunt out in a glass ashtray with the gentlemen's club name and logo on it. He then made his way upon the stage and sat down. Billie hung her whip around his neck. She handcuffed his wrists behind his back with a pair of pink furry handcuffs. At that moment, Usher's *Can U Handle It* pumped from the speakers, and the spotlight shone down on Billie and God, leaving everyone else in the shadows of the dimly lit establishment.

*I think that you should know*
*You're doing the most, sugar*
*So don't worry 'bout the situation*
*I'd never let you go*

Keeping her eyes on God, and her hand on his chair, Billie circled the chair slowly, doing a complete 360-degree turn. She then sat on his lap and threw her arms around his neck, putting her face dangerously close to his face. The moment she did, God basked in her enchanting perfume, loving the fragrance of it. Billie stared into his eyes and ground her hips, feeling his dick bulge in his jeans. God gasped and so did she, feeling each other growing more and more aroused through the friction of her clothing against his.

"You like that, daddy?" Billie asked him, bouncing up and down upon him.

"I love it, ma." God stuck his tongue out of his mouth, licking her up her neck and around her chin. He then licked along her collar bone gently. He just knew she was going to tell him to stop, but surprisingly she didn't. It was against the rules to touch the girls at the club. He knew this, but he didn't give a rat's ass. He was a boss-ass nigga, and boss-ass niggaz did what they wanted, not what they were told. Straight like that!

Billie threw her head back and leaned almost all of the way to the floor, hair dangling below her. She saw every one inside the club from this upside down view. When she brought herself back up, she placed her hands on God's knees and wrapped her thick legs around his shoulders. She humped her pussy into his face; driving the audience of men wild and making God wish his hands were free of those fur handcuffs; because if they were, he would have fucked her right there on that stage.

Dollar after dollar was thrown on the stage, by men that wished they were in God's shoes, personally enjoying the show being put on by the amazing Snake Eyez, aka Billie Bad Ass. Billie brought her legs down and spun around, so that her back would be facing God. She grabbed his ankles and leaned forward so her ass would be tilted up in his face. She started making her ass cheeks dance, one at a time, and then she began popping her pussy. Next, Billie brought her ass back down upon his lap, grinding into his manhood. Feeling her pussy tingling, Billie moved faster and faster. She found the moisture building between her legs while God held his masculine frame of mind. He acted like he wasn't fazed by her performance, but he most definitely was. He just wasn't about to let her know she had him going like she was. He was a boss-ass nigga, so he couldn't allow himself to get worked up over pussy. Billie continued to whip her sexual prowess on God, until she had an orgasm and made an ugly face.

Billie leaned back against God, breathing heavily and sweating. She rested her cheek against his. She brought her arm around his head and held him close. He was looking at her like he was *that* nigga. She and he looked into each other's eyes, and then it happened, they kissed. They kissed passionately like they were longtime lovers.

*We gon' lay it out*
*We gon' tear it up*
*Baby, can you handle it?*
*I can handle it*
*I can go there, baby, with you*

The song went off. DJ Flip spoke over the microphone. "Everyone, give a round of applause for Snake Eyez!"

The men in the audience rose to their feet, applauding, hooting, hollering and throwing more money. Billie got off of God and came around his back, un-cuffing him. She then took the leather whip from around his neck, and sauntered to the back of the stage, heading for the curtains. Her chunky butt swung from left to right, enticing everyone watching her as she made her exit.

\*\*\*

Billie emerged from the back of The Pussy Kat Club, switching hands with her purse as she walked towards her car. God spotted her while he was leant up against the side of the strip club, talking to some of his goons, indulging in a blunt. He blew the last of the smoke out of his mouth, passed the bleezy to one of his goons, and headed in Billie's direction. Unbeknownst to him, she smiled to herself, knowing she had his full attention. Still, that didn't slow her stride. She continued towards her vehicle, like she didn't know he was on her.

God jogged after her and called out her name. By the time he caught up with her, she was secure behind the wheel of her car. She was about to start her whip up, until he knocked on the driver's window and garnered her attention. She looked at him, and he signaled for her to let her window down. She obliged him.

"What's up, love? I know you not finna walk away from yo destiny?"

*Damn, this nigga fine ass fuck! Baby can get it all day long,* Billie thought to herself. *Chill out, Billie, can't be acting all thirsty for the nigga. Play it cool, like you'd do with any other nigga. You can't act too eager and blow yo mothafucking cover now.*

"My destiny, huh?" Billie cracked a smile. "What makes you so sure that chu my destiny?"

"Well, fate put us here together tonight. So I know it was my destiny to meet chu. I don't believe in coincidences, you feel me?"

"Tell me something, uhhhhh—" she looked at him, waiting for him to tell her his name.

"God. My name is God."

"Now I know good and goddamn well yo momma didn't name you God. What's the name of yo birth certificate?"

God looked at her for a minute, debating on whether or not he should tell her his government name.

"Kyree. Kyree Purdy." He gave up his name like he hated to do so, and he did hate to do so.

"Kyree, huh? I like that. It's very strong, hood, and sexy."

God smiled, and his cheeks dimpled.

*Oh, my god, nigga, I'm ready to have yo baby witcho fine-ass!*

"What's yo name, ma? I mean, since we dropping govs and shit?"

"My name's Billie."

"Billie, huh?"

"Yeah, my daddy wanted a boy, but luckily for him he got something better." She capped with a smile.

"Is that right? Check lil' baby out."

God and Billie shot the shit a while longer before she was programming her digits into his cellular.

"So, I'ma get up witchu later, alright?" God said to her, kissing her hand.

"Well, aren't chu the smooth one!"

"I wouldn't say I'm smooth. I just know how to conduct myself when a lady is in my presence."

"Really? So you look at me as a lady and not some fucking sex object?" She looked at him like, *Nigga, come on now,* angling her head to the side.

"Look, you're a woman, an attractive one at that. So when I look at you, I do see someone I'd like to have sex with in the future. But as of right now, I am focused more on getting to know you as a person. The sex will just be a bonus."

*If this nigga is not strapped with game—Boyyyyy, I tell you.*

"So, you not tripping on me showing my tits and ass for money?"

"Nah, I know how to separate the person from their profession. Besides, I know you not tryna be a stripper forever, right?" He looked at her like, *Ma, I know you got bigger plans for the future.*

"Hell nah. This shit is just to pay the bills. I plan on going to school for cosmetology and opening up my own hair salon."

"See, I knew you were my destiny."

"How so, handsome?"

"The woman God wants me to be with is groomed for boss status."

"Sho' you right."

God smiled, patted the rooftop of her car, and walked away. Billie went to start up her car, but the engine wouldn't turn over. The sound of it stalling caused God to turn around with a furrowed forehead. He walked over to the car and asked Billie what was wrong?

"I don't know. I tried to start it up, but the engine wouldn't turn over."

"Do me a favor, pop the trunk for me."

Billie did like he commanded and he lifted the hood, looking things over. He fiddled with something and told Billie to fire up the engine again, but the mothafucka wouldn't turn on. Noting this, God let down the hood of the car and walked over to Billie.

"Look, I don't know what's wrong with yo whip, but I'ma calla potna of mine so he can pick up yo car. I'll have 'em take it to his shop and check it out."

"Listen, I really don't have the money to pay for whatever is going on with my—"

God put up his hand, which stopped her words short. "I'ma take care of everything, don't even wet it. I'ma call you an Uber to take you home too. You know what, as a matter of fact, I'ma do you one better, since there's a lotta weirdoes that be driving for Uber and shit, I'ma calla limousine service to pick you up and take you home. I'll hit chu up tomorrow afternoon to let chu know what's going on with your whip, cool?"

"I appreciate it. But for real, you really don't have to do that for me."

"I know I don't. But I want to. I'm in the Christmas spirits." He smiled, then pulled out his cell phone. He hit up a limousine service, and a stretch Mercedes Benz pulled up fast. "There you ride go, right there." He nodded to the Mercedes, just as the blue-eyed, Caucasian chauffeur hopped out and opened the back door of the luxury vehicle.

When Billie looked over and saw the limousine, she opened the door of her car, and God helped her out by grabbing her hand. She adjusted the strap of the knapsack over her shoulder, and made her way across the street, sitting down in the backseat. She smiled and waved at God, before the chauffeur closed the door behind her. He then got in the limousine and drove off. As he left the scene, the tow truck was pulling up, and God was making his way towards it, flagging the driver behind the wheel down.

***

Billie laid in bed, snoring softly, arms and leg twisted in awkward directions. The slight openings of the blinds let the bright rays of the sunshine through, the rays beaming on her face and the upper half of her body. It wasn't long before her nose and eyelids started twitching, as she heard the vibration and ringing of her cellular phone from where it lay on the dresser. Her eyelids fluttered like the wings of a butterfly, and she looked over at her cell phone, face scrunched up, vision blurry. The device stopped ringing, but she went ahead and sat up in bed. Throwing her head back, yawning, she stretched her arms, hearing her bones cracking, popping and adjusting. Right then, the cell phone vibrated and rang again. She peeked over at the display of her cell phone, and saw God's name and digits on it. She answered the device, yawning again and saying *excuse me*.

"Hello?" she spoke into the jack.

"What's up, ma? I'm outside witcho car."

"Huh? How you know where I live?"

"You in the book, slim. Come outside."

At that moment, Annabelle emerged into her bedroom in her Powerpuff Girls pajamas, toting a stuffed teddy bear. She twisted her knuckle at the corner of her eye, sounding groggy as she spoke.

"Good morning, mommy." Annabelle walked over to her mother.

"Good morning, beautiful." Billie picked her up and sat her on her lap, kissed her on the cheek. "Where are you?" she said to God over the phone.

"I'm right outside, standing on the curb."

Billie picked up Annabelle and put her on her hip, walking her over to her window which was covered by blinds. She peeked out from between the blinds, peering out below at God. He was smiling up at her and waving his hand.

"Oh, my God, you're really here?" Billie's eyes bulged with surprise. She thought God was bullshitting her about being outside of her house, but he wasn't. He was dead ass serious. "Look, God, I appreciate chu fixing my car, but you shouldn't have come over to my house. I don't bring my daughter around men I don't know I'm seriously dating or not."

"Well, technically, we aren't dating yet. We're just friends right now. And I brought my daughter with me, too."

"Really? I didn't know you hadda lil' girl."

"Now you do. And I'm sure she'd like to meet yo lil' mama. Hold on."

Right then, Billie overheard God say something to someone, and then a little girl came on the telephone.

"Hello, Ms. Billie. My name is Charity. Can you please come outside so I can meet you and your daughter?"

"Awwww," Billie made a face like, *She's so precious.* She hated to deny the little girl a chance of meeting her. And God did have a point. They weren't technically dating yet; they were still just friends. So there wasn't really a problem with her daughter meeting God and his little girl. "Tell yo daddy me and baby girl will be down in a second, okay?"

"Okay. We'll see you then."

Billie disconnected the call. She then slipped a hoodie on over her head, and placed her feet in a pair of lady Air Max sneakers. She had her daughter throw on a jacket and stuff her bare feet inside of her light-up sneakers. Annabelle grabbed her mother's hand and allowed her to lead her outside, where God and Charity were awaiting them. Charity and Annabelle smiled big when they saw each other. Billie introduced the girls; thereafter, she introduced her daughter to God.

"Hello there, lil' lady. It's a pleasure to meet chu." God smiled as he held Annabelle's hand, leaning downward and kissing it.

"It's a pleasure to meet chu too, God." Annabelle smiled and giggled.

"You know you're just as pretty as your momma?"

"Thank you. I get it from my mommy."

"No doubt." God looked Billie over like she was the most beautiful woman he'd ever laid his eyes on. She smiled and blushed.

"Come on, Ms. Billie—let me show you to your car." Charity took Billie by the hand, leading her over to her car. God came behind Billie, placing his hands over her eyes.

"Wait a minute, what's going on?"

"It's a surprise," Charity told her.

"Oh, goodie, mommy, I just love surprises!" Annabelle clapped her hands excitedly as she walked behind her mother, God and Charity.

"What's the surprise? You just got my car fixed."

"Something like that. Here we are. Now, on the count of three, I'm gonna take my hands from your eyes. One, two, three!"

God took his hands away from Billie's eyes, and she jumped excitedly. Her eyes and mouth were wide open. She was greeted by a brand new cocaine-white 2019 BMW 5 Series 530i with blood-red interior and matching red rims.

"Oh, my God! Oh, my God, this is mine? This is my car?" Billie asked God, holding him by his shoulders. A smirking God nodded. "Well, what happened to my old car?"

"Well, it needed quite a bit of work, so I got rid of it. I said, fuck it, lemme gon' buy lil' mama something new and fly. So, here we are. You wanna take her for a spin?" God held up the key to the luxury vehicle, wiggling it.

"Hell yeah, I wanna take her for a spin." Billie snatched the key and went to run for her new car, but she doubled back. She narrowed her eyelids at him and said, with one of her hands on her hip, "What's the catch? And don't tell me there's none 'cause there's always one."

God threw up his hands and said, "There's no catch. I'm just helping outta friend. We're friends right?" He outstretched his hand.

"Yeah, we're friends." She shook his hand. "Now, y'all come on so I can take my new baby for a ride."

Billie ran over to the BMW and jumped in, firing it up as everyone else was getting in. She looked through her rearview mirror, and then adjusted the side view mirror. Once she saw that no one was coming, she hit her turning signal and pulled out of the parking space into traffic. Billie whipped her car through the streets, banging Moneybagg Yo. The girls rode in the back, playing patty cake, and got to know one another. While this was going on, God was riding shotgun and telling Billie about everything the luxury vehicle had to offer. A second later, Billie was jumping on the freeway, bringing the car up to top speed, punching out. The music was blasting, and the wind was whipping through everyone's hair and ruffling their clothing.

"This mothafucka hard, right?" God looked at Billie.

"I love this car. Thank you, thank you, thank you." Billie smiled at him.

"You're welcome." He smiled back, placing his hand on her thigh. She looked down at his hand. Thinking that she wasn't feeling him, he moved his hand and she placed it back. They exchanged smiles.

***

Billie whipped back to her apartment. She couldn't stop looking back at her brand new ass car and thanking God. God and Charity walked Billie and Annabelle to the door of her unit. Billie opened the door of her apartment and turned around to them.

"I'll see you later, best friend," Annabelle told Charity.

"Okay, best friend." Charity hugged Annabelle and kissed her on the cheek.

"Awwww, that's so sweet." Billie looked at God's daughter, as she hugged Annabelle.

God smiled at Charity, as she and her new best friend held hands inside of the hallway.

"They've really taken to each other, huh?" God said to Billie.

Looking at the little girls, Billie said: "Yeah. They really have. My baby is always talking about how she wants a lil' sister."

"Hey, what chu got up for the night?" God asked Billie.

"Nothing much. Why, what do you have going?"

"I was thinking maybe you and the princess would like to go ice skating."

"Oooooh, mommy, say yes, please. I'd love to go ice skating!" Annabelle pulled on the sleeve of her mother's jacket, causing her to smile.

"Oh, please, say yes, Ms. Billie," Charity begged with her fingers interlocked.

"What's up, lil' mama, you rolling or what?" God asked.

"Yeah, we're going," Billie responded.

Her answer was music to the girls' ears. Annabelle and Charity hugged each other, and jumped up and down, excitedly.

"Me and my best friend are going skating! Me and my best friend going skating! Me and my best friend going skating!" the girls sang over and over again, their arms over each other's shoulders.

"Look at them—they're something else," Billie said.

"Yeah, our baby girls." God glanced at his Rolex and said, "Look, I gotta get up outta here. I gotta few moves I needa make, but I'ma swing back through here 'round eight o'clock. Okay?"

"Okay."

God gave her his cheek to kiss. When she leaned forward to kiss him, he turned his head and her lips fell against his lips, kissing him. Billie smiled and blushed. The girls laughed at her.

"You think you slick, huh?" Billie asked.

"As a pig in dookie. We'll see you ladies at eight tonight." God took his daughter by the hand and led her away. Charity turned around as she was being led away, waving goodbye to Annabelle and Billie. Billie and Annabelle waved back before retreating to their apartment. God and Charity went outside, and hopped into the limousine he'd called up for them on their way back over to Billie's crib.

# Chapter 7

### *Later that night*

Annabelle sat on her Barbie bed, combing the hair of her Barbie doll while her mother, Billie, went through the rack of clothes inside her closet. She was trying to find her daughter something to wear that night to the ice skating ring.

"Mommy, what're you doing?" Annabelle asked, focused on combing her doll's hair. She didn't even look up to see what her mother was doing, but she knew she was inside her closet.

"I'm trying to find you something to wear, baby girl. How about this? It's cute." A smiling Billie turned around with a full royal blue and pink hooded Nike sweat suit.

Annabelle sat her doll and comb down on her bed. She then hopped off her bed and walked over to Billie. She massaged her chin, as she held onto the leg of the sweat pants, wearing a face of concentration.

"Hmmmm," Annabelle said, tilting her head from left to right. She was thinking about how she felt about the outfit her mother had picked out for her. "I don't like it. May I pick out my own clothes to wear on your date?"

"My date?" Billie gave her a side eye before placing the outfit back on the rack. "What makes you think this is a date?"

"I see the way you look at your—" she made the quotes with her fingers. "Friend. You really like him. I can tell."

"Oh, yeah?" Billie cracked a grin and folded her arms across her breasts. She then stepped aside to allow her daughter a clear path to the closet, watching her try to find herself something to wear that night.

"Unh huh," Annabelle said going through the clothes. Once she found what she wanted to wear, she gave it to her mother and then started searching for sneakers to wear. "I can see it now. First he's your friend, then your boyfriend, and then he's your husband. Once you get married, Charity and I will be sisters. Then I'll have my real daddy, a step daddy—and then, maybe one day—a baby brother, like I always wanted."

Billie smiled hard at what her daughter had said. "You're a trip, lil' girl, you know that?"

"Yep. Can you iron that for me, please?" Annabelle pointed at the outfit her mother was holding.

"Sure. Gemme a kiss." She leaned forward and Annabelle kissed her.

Annabelle hopped onto her Barbie bed and started combing her doll's hair again. While she was busy doing this, Billie walked out of her bedroom and into her own. When Billie returned to her bedroom, she started ironing the outfit her daughter wanted to wear that night. Once she was finished, she ironed the clothes she would wear that night as well. Once she was done, she took her daughter the outfit. When she returned to Annabelle's bedroom, she found her lying on her stomach, legs up in the air, writing something down a notepad. While Annabelle was writing, she was singing a song from the animated cartoon *Aladdin*.

"What chu do, baby girl?" a frowning Billie asked Annabelle, as she laid her outfit down on the bed.

"I am writing down all of the things I want Santa to bring me for Christmas, mommy." Annabelle continued to sing as she wrote down the items she wanted for Christmas.

Billie looked over her daughter's shoulder, seeing all of the gifts your average little girl would want for Christmas. But there was one that caught her off guard. It was the sixth item listed on the piece of paper. Below number five—which was for her daddy, Joaquin, to be released from jail. Number six was a family. Billie's eyes threatened to drip tears. Right before the teardrops could fall, Billie wiped her eyes with the back of her fist. She then kissed Annabelle on top of her head and told her, "I love you."

"I love you too, mommy." Annabelle continued to sing and write.

"I'm gonna go take a shower and get dressed. Once you finish your Christmas list, you do the same."

"Okay."

Billie walked back inside her bedroom and shut the door behind her. She placed her back against it, bowed her head and started crying, teardrops falling from her eyes.

*Oh, my God! Am I a bad mom? I couldn't give her the family she wanted, and now I can't afford to get her Christmas gifts. Fuck that!*

Billie looked up with pink, dripping eyes. She wiped her eyes with the palms of her hands and sniffled.

*Once I smoke this nigga, I'll have enough dough to give baby girl all of the gifts she wants for Christmas. And then I can see who the fuck this ho ass nigga is snitching on Joaquin and get his ass faded too. I'ma get lil' mama all she wants. And if that means, some other lil' girl going without her father, then fuck it, so be it!*

Billie pulled her black .32 pistol with the silencer attached to its barrel from underneath the mattress and aimed it at the lamp sitting across the room. She imagined the lamp was God, and pretended to pull the trigger. Billie then took a deep breath and lowered her banger.

*Damn, when the time comes, am I really going to be able to pull the trigga though? I'm really feeling this nigga. I mean, I'm feeling 'em a lot, a lot. I know it's early, but I*

Tranay Adams

*could really see myself being with him. On some forever type shit. I know it sounds crazy, but I've never felt like this before. Not even with Joaquin. That's the coldest part! I know what I gotta do on the account of my baby girl. I love her to death. But in making sure that she's happy, will I be throwing away my own?* Billie stashed her silenced pistol back where she'd gotten it. She then stripped down and headed into the bathroom conjoined to her master bedroom. She turned on the shower water and adjusted its temperature to her liking, before stepping inside the tub and lathering up.

*When the time comes, I'm gonna have to do what I have to do. No matter if I like it or not. When Annabelle was born, I vowed to place her happiness in front of my own. I just hope what's in my mind doesn't deter my heart. Please, God, help me do what's right.*

***

"I look like a straight up New York nigga in this fit—but fuck it—I'm dope boy fresh out this bitch," God said, as he stood before the mirror attached to his nightstand, looking himself over. He was in a navy blue NY fitted cap, a hoodie with a puffy vest over it, and construction Timbs, with untied shoestrings.

Hearing his cell phone vibrate and ring stole God's attention. He looked at his dresser and found his device's screen lighting up. The letter M was on the display, so he already knew who was banging his line. He answered with the quickness.

"Hold on for a second, my nigga." God pressed his cellular to his chest and walked to his daughter's bedroom, opening the door. When he peered inside, he saw her fully clothed for the night's festivities, having a tea party with her Barbie dolls and stuffed animals.

"Would you like some tea, Mr. Beasley?" Charity asked one of the stuffed animals. "I don't mind if I do, Charity," she said in a manly British accent, making it sound as though that was the reponse of 'Mr. Beasley'

God smiled, seeing his daughter playing in her bedroom. Before he left out, he heard her say, "How about you, Mrs. Crompton, would you like some tea to go with your cookies?"

God shut the door behind him and journeyed down the hallway, pressing the cell phone to his ear, saying, "Go 'head." He listened to what he was being told, as he turned the corner inside his bedroom, pacing the floor as he talked. "So, that bitch-ass nigga is up there, huh?" He massaged his chin as he thought, listening to what he was being told again. "Mothafucka got the nerve to put money on my head? I got chu. All that means is, his ass heard about ol' boy and now he's shook. I tell you what. You do the same. I know yo rate. Peace." He disconnected the call and stuck it inside of his pocket. Next, he took his God .45 automatic handgun from underneath his mattress and tucked it on his waistline.

God journeyed out of his bedroom, and walked inside Charity's bedroom. She was still sipping tea with her toys.

"Hey, baby girl, you ready to go?" God asked enthusiastically, as he rubbed his hands together.

"Yep." She rose to her feet and grabbed her jacket, slipping it on. God walked over to her and zipped it up. He then held her by the front of her jacket, rubbing his nose against hers, which caused her to smile. He then pecked her lips and then her forehead. Once he stood upright, he took her by the hand and they headed out of her bedroom. God flipped off the light switch as they came out of her bedroom, heading into the living room. As they crossed the living room floor, Charity's eyes came across several portraits of her mother which were all on the mantle.

"Wait a minute, daddy. We can't go without saying goodbye to mommy first." Charity stopped her father and walked over to the mantle. She motioned for her father to come over and take the biggest portrait of her mother down for her. He walked over and took the portrait down, handing it to her.

Charity looked at the portrait, smiling from ear to ear. "Hey, Mommy, I hope you're having a fun time in heaven. Daddy and I are going out tonight to ice skate with our new friends. We'll be back later. I'll see you when we come back. I love you so much. Muah!" She kissed the portrait and outstretched it to her father. He took it. "Tell mommy you love her, too."

"Hey, baby," God began, staring down at the portrait of his late wife. He couldn't help the tears that accumulated in his eyes. Ever since she'd left his life, he'd been sick without her. It seemed as if every hour of every day, his thoughts constantly stayed on her. "I love—" he took the time to gather himself, as he found his voice cracking. "I love you, and I miss you. I miss you so very, very much, sweetheart."

"Don't cry, daddy." Charity ran out of the living and into the kitchen, returning with a balled up paper towel. She motioned for her father to kneel down, and he did. She then dabbed his eyes dry. "It's gonna be okay, daddy. Mommy is okay. She's in heaven with the Lord and all of his angels, and they're looking out for us down here. Remember? You remember when you told me that? It's true, right?"

God took a deep breath and pulled himself together. He knew he was weak right then. He understood that his daughter needed him to be strong for both of them. If she saw him in his current state any longer, she'd begin to fall apart. And he loved her so much he didn't like her to see him in this emotional state. "Yeah, that's right. Mommy is in heaven with God and the angels, looking out for us."

Charity finished drying her father's eyes and balled up the paper towels. She then kissed him on the cheek and hugged him.

"I love you, daddy."

"I love you, too, princess," God replied. He then stood upright and took her hand, continuing out of the mansion.

\*\*\*

God dipped by Billie's crib to pick up her and her daughter. They then swung by the ice skating ring, but found that it was closed down due to remodeling. Disappointment was written on the girls' faces, until God told them that they'd grab McDonald's and go see the Christmas lights that everyone had on their homes in Beverly Hills. The girls were clapping and hopping around in their seats when they heard they'd get Mickey D's. They both loved McDonald's food, especially their strawberry shakes. They couldn't wait to see the light show either. Charity told Annabelle about how her father had taken her to see the lights last year in this area with nice big houses. She then asked her father if he was going to take them to that same neighborhood.

"You got it, baby girl," God said over his shoulder. He then looked to Billie. "Hey, see if you can find us some Christmas music to listen to."

Billie flipped through the channels until she found a Christmas song by Frank Sinatra, *Have yourself a Merry Little Christmas*.

*Have yourself a merry little Christmas*
*Let your heart be light*
*From now on our troubles*
*Will be out of sight*

God dipped by McDonald's drive thru. He ordered himself a Big Mac combo; Billie, a Fillet-O-Fish combo; and the girls, Happy Meals, together with their strawberry shakes. Once he paid for everyone's food, God passed out the bags. The girls didn't waste any time opening up their bags and stuffing their mouths with fries. Billie took a bite of her fish sandwich, then she took a sip of her Coca Cola. From the corner of her eye, she saw God eyeing her sandwich. She smiled.

"You wanna bite?" Billie asked him.

"Yeah. If you don't mind, that sandwich looks good than a mothafucka."

Billie let God get a bite of fish sandwich. As he munched his bite, a smile spread across his face. Billie, smiling, wiped the tartar sauce from the corner of his mouth and kissed him on the cheek.

"Is it good, bae? I mean, God?" Billie asked.

"Yeah. It's good. I don't normally mess with fish, but that sandwich is the truth." He grabbed a few napkins from out of the brown McDonald's bag and wiped his mouth with it. "Now that that's outta the way, did you just call me, bae?"

"Nah, nah, I didn't say that."

"Yes, you did, mommy, 'cause Charity and I heard you." Annabelle put her mother on blast.

"Mmmmmhmmm." Charity nodded and ate another fry.

"How you just gon' give yo momma up like that, Annabelle? You cold." Billie chuckled as she looked back at her daughter.

Annabelle shrugged and said, "Yeah, well, he bought me McDonald's, mommy." She popped another fry into her mouth.

"Lil' girl, you gave me up for a Happy Meal?"

"Unh huh." She nodded.

"So, you love Mickey D's more than yo momma?"

"Mommy, please don't make me answer that."

God busted up laughing.

"What chu laughing at?" Billie playfully punched him. "Just admit to what chu said."

Billie took a deep breath and said, "Alright. I said, bae."

"Now, see, was it that hard?" He grasped her hand and kissed it. She smiled hard.

As God continued to drive, Billie focused her attention out of the passenger window. The smile disappeared from her face once she remembered she'd eventually have to murk God.

*Damn, I'm really gonna have to go through with it,* Billie thought to herself.

Seeing the despair written across Billie's face through her reflection in the passenger window caused a line to form across God's forehead. He found himself wondering what was troubling her.

"Is everything okay, ma?" God questioned with concern.

Billie mustered up a fake smile and said, "Yeah. I'm okay." She took another bite of her sandwich.

"You sure?"

"Unh huh." Billie nodded with a smile and gave him another bite of the fish sandwich.

"Alright, ladies, the light show is coming up," God announced to everyone, as he made a right at the corner. As soon as he did, they were bombarded with colorful lights which were on everyone's house, trees and bushes. God coasted down the block, like his vehicle was in a parade, trying to make sure that everyone got a good look at the lit up houses. The colorfully lit houses shone on the windshield and passenger windows of his car. By this time, Annabelle and Charity were done eating; their faces were plastered to the windows, taking in the amazing, breath-taking sight. All the while, Christmas music pumped from out of the vehicle's speakers, softly.

*Here we are as in olden days*
*Happy golden days of yore*
*Faithful friends who are dear to us*
*Gather near to us, once more*

"Mommy, look, look!" Annabelle tapped her mother rapidly on the shoulder and pointed at the house that had her and Charity's undivided attention.

"Look at the house Annabelle's pointing at, daddy, it's beautiful," Charity told God as she stared at the well-lit house. The house was as big as a mansion, and every inch of it was covered in lights.

"Wow!—That's amazing," Billie told her daughter, in reference to the house.

God finally looked at the house. "I know they light bill high as a mothafucka, boy."

Billie laughed her ass off and said, "Leave it to black folks to say something like that."

God shrugged and said, "I'm just saying. I'd hate to see that bill."

God took the girls down six more blocks in Beverly Hills, all of which had houses that had lights up for Christmas. There were other families out on the streets in their cars, enjoying the fantastic sights just as they were, finding themselves amazed.

Once the last block was spun, God noted how quiet the car had become; so he adjusted the rearview mirror. He looked up in it and saw that Annabelle and Charity were laid against one another, eyelids shut, mouth open, snoring softly asleep.

"Look at the girls," God nudged Billie, but she didn't respond. When he looked over at her, she was knocked out asleep, too. A smile spread across his lips, as he admired how beautiful she was—even in sleep. He kissed her tenderly on the forehead and rolled up the windows, turning on the heater so that it could warm inside. Afterwards, he turned the stereo onto Meek Mill's *Oodles O' Noodles Babies* track, and continued to drive, nodding.

*I ain't have nobody to give me no hope*
*I hope my momma ain't doin' no coke*
*I used to wish that my daddy was livin'*
*I had a dream that I seen him as ghost*

\*\*\*

God pulled up outside Billie's apartment building and woke her up. She sat up in her seat, frowning and stretching her arms and legs.

"Man, what time is it?" Billie asked him.

God looked at his Rolex and told her the time. "It's ten thirty-five."

Billie peered into the backseat and smiled when she saw the girls were fast asleep.

"Look at our lil' angels—Aren't they beautiful?" Billie said, eyes lingering on Annabelle and Charity.

"Yeah. They really are." God looked into the backseat.

"Thank you for taking us out tonight. Annabelle and I really enjoyed ourselves." Billie took his hand into her lap and caressed it, staring into his eyes lovingly.

"No thanks needed. It was all my pleasure." He brushed her hair out of her face, and stared deep into her eyes. "You wanna know something crazy?"

"Sure."

"We haven't been kicking it two days, and already I can see myself fucking witchu like that."

"Fucking with me like that, how?" he asked curiously.

Billie's cheeks turned red with embarrassment, and she looked down at his hand, continuously caressing it. "Never mind. I'd be doing too much if I said all of what was on my mind."

"I hear you. But sometimes you gotta just say fuck it, and put cho self out there. You know, see what happens. You never know." He rubbed her cheek with the side of his fist.

Billie nodded her understanding of where God was coming from and then said, "Well, what I meant to say was, I can see myself being in a relationship witchu, getting married, having our own children together and growing old. I know I'm wilding 'cause it's so early, but—"

Billie was suddenly cut off by God turning her to face him by her chin and kissing her lingeringly, deeply, and passionately. He then pulled back, and kissed her on the lips one more time. "You not wilding, slim. I see all of that you see, and more. And it's nice to know that chu feel the same."

"Really?" she asked him with a smile.

"Facts." He smiled back at her.

Billie repositioned herself in the front seat and turned to him. "Sooooo, when the next time you tryna hang out?"

"Shit, tomorrow. How about we hit up the Santa Monica Pier?"

"Okay. The pier it is."

"Alright then. It's a date."

"It's a date."

Billie kissed him and hopped out of the car. God hopped out behind her and scooped up Annabelle, handing her off to Billie. They kissed again and he stood beside his whip, watching Billie carry her daughter inside the tenement, until she was out of his sight. Afterwards, God jumped behind the wheel of his ride and peeled off, heading back home.

\*\*\*

### Two weeks before Christmas

God, Billie and their girls had been kicking it real tough. They'd all gotten to know one another very well. They'd all become inseparable since their first initial meeting. God and Billie got to know one another on a more personal level. God finally told her that he was a dope boy. He thought that it was going to be a deal breaker for her, but to his surprise she wasn't tripping off of it. What he didn't know was, if he could accept her being a stripper then she could accept the fact that he was a trapper. Anyway, God and Billie seemed to be having a ball with one another. Until one night, when they were all gathered at his house, watching Christmas movies and sipping egg nog, and Billie got a call.

"Who is that, ma?" God asked Billie from where he was sitting up in his bed. The girls were at the foot of the bed, with their chin resting on their fists, watching *Jingle All The Way*.

Billie's face frowned up when she pulled her cell phone out of her purse and saw Kershawn's face and number on its screen. Seeing her uncle's face zapped her back to reality. It made her realize that she'd been living in a fantasy world. She'd been living in a world where none of her problems existed, where she and her daughter were truly happy. But all of that had changed the moment her cellular rang. Billie was supposed to have knocked God's head off already, but she had failed to do so.

"It's, uh, it's my Uncle Kershawn. Gemme a second, I gotta take this, okay?" Billie slid off of the bed and headed for the door.

"Okay. Take however long you need," God told her.

From the corner of her eye, Annabelle saw her mother stepping away. She looked to the door to see Billie attempting to leave.

"Mommy, where are you going?" Annabelle asked with a frown.

"Out into the hall to talk to your uncle," Billie said over her shoulder, with her cellular pressed to her breasts. She then blew Annabelle a kiss and continued out of the bedroom, pulling the door shut behind her. She walked away from God's bedroom door, so he wouldn't be able to overhear her conversation. "What's up, unc?" Billie pressed her cell phone to her ear, and leaned her shoulder against the hallway wall, focusing her attention on God's bedroom door.

"You finish yo food yet?" Kershawn asked, referring to Billie's killing of God.

"Not yet."

"Well, you needa finish that plate tonight. Or I'ma give it to someone else."

"I'm hungry, so I'ma eat it."

"Good."

Kershawn disconnected the call and Billie returned to God's master bedroom, smiling.

"What's up with unc?" God asked her.

"Nothing. Just wanted to see if I was coming by for Christmas," Billie said with a straight face. She dropped her cell phone into her purse and snuggled under God. He placed his arm around her and kissed her on top of the head. They focused their attention back on the television. Billie found her eyes pooling with tears, thinking about what she had to do that night. She knew she had to do it though, for the sake of her daughter.

\*\*\*

The girls ended up falling asleep on the show they were watching. So God tucked Charity in for the night and carried a sleeping Annabelle out to Billie's BMW. He placed her into the backseat, buckled her in and kissed her on the forehead goodbye. He then dipped his head into the driver's window and kissed Billie on the lips.

"Call me once you get in so I know you got in safe, okay?" God told her.

"Okay. I love you." Billie eyes bulged, and she smacked her hand over her mouth. She hated herself for saying that aloud. *You stupid, bitch, why'd you tell 'em that? He's gon' think you sprung off the D. And he only fucked one time. Fuck!* "I'm sorry. I didn't mean that, it just slipped out."

Grinning, God said, "I know. So that means it came from the heart." He stuck his head inside the window. "Don't worry, I love you too, ma." He kissed her romantically. And once he pulled back from her, she was smiling. Suddenly, that smile vanished and her eyes pooled with tears that eventually went jetting down her cheeks. He frowned up, seeing her cry, and wiped her dripping eyes with his thumbs. "What's the matter, Billie?"

Billie shook her head and said, "Nothing. It's just that—I never felt this way about anyone before."

Billie was lying through her fucking teeth. She was crying because she was in love with God and—unfortunately—she was going to have to kill him that night. Once she did the deed, she didn't have any idea how she was going to be able to live with herself. That is, if she could live with herself, knowing she'd laid down the nigga she was in love with.

God chopped it up with Billie for a while longer, before kissing her goodbye and heading inside the house. As soon as he crossed the threshold into his plush home, he got another call from 'M' telling him that the dude he'd put the hit out on was going to get taken care of real soon. The 'hitman' was just earning his friendship to lower his guard, and once he'd gotten it down, he was going to make him a memory.

God went inside the kitchen and poured himself up a half glass of Hennessy. He made his way across the living room floor, crossing the seven-foot-tall white Christmas tree, which was inside the corner, decorated in royal blue and silver adornments. The colorful lights surrounding the great, big tree flashed on and off, their lights stabbing at God. God picked up one of the many portraits of his deceased wife. He took a sip of his drink and smiled at her, kissing the portrait.

"No matter how close it seems I am getting with another woman, I promise I'll never love anyone as much as I love you. That's on our daughter." He kissed the portrait again and sat it back down on its mantle. He then walked back across the living room floor. Stopping at the entrance of the hallway, he looked back at the portrait he'd just sat down, smiled and journeyed down the corridor. Returning to his bedroom, he put the TV on Netflix and searched the content until he found *Scarface*. He started up the show and watched it, sipping his drink casually.

\*\*\*

Billie dropped Annabelle off at Kershawn's house. He stood in the doorway with his arms folded across his chest, watching her get dressed in an all-black outfit for the night's mission. Once Billie pinned her hair up, she secured the small throwing knives on her waistline and up her sleeves. She then gave herself the once-over and took a deep breath, preparing herself for the night's assignment. Once she figured she'd gotten her mind right, she headed out of the bathroom, but her uncle stopped her. He could see the pain in her eyes, so he hugged her and rubbed her back. She shuddered and cried in his arms.

"Shhhhh. There, there, there it's gonna be all right." Kershawn tightened his embrace and kissed her on the side of the head. He then held her at arm's length and tilted her chin upwards, so that she'd be looking in his eyes. "Listen, you don't have to go through with this. Like I said, I can give you the money to take care of you and—"

Billie's eyes dripped tears as she placed her gloved finger to Kershawn's lips, saying, "I'm going to do what I have to do to provide for my daughter and I. If this nigga gotta go in order for her to eat and have her father home, then so be it. Now, hug me again please."

Kershawn hugged Billie again, rubbing his hand up and down her back. He knew exactly how she felt about the man he'd hired her to kill, and how hard it was going to be for her to carry out his murder. He also knew that he couldn't convince her to just take the money from him to handle all of her bills and shit, because she wasn't going take it. So the best he could do was, let her follow up with her decision and pray that she could live with the choice she made once it was all said and done.

Billie cried long and hard in Kershawn's arms, tears soaking through his shirt. Kershawn continued to comfort her, and in doing so he felt himself growing teary eyed. He loved Billie like a daughter. Hell, he'd raised her by himself; so, of course, he felt some kind of way about her grieving.

### Forty minutes later

Billie pulled up on a residential block and walked a block over, stealing a four-door '99 Grand Prix. She drove the vehicle over to God's house and parked in the alley. She then scaled the gate of a house where no one appeared to be living. Afterwards, she crept up the driveway, ran across the street and climbed up the side of his house. Making it upon the rooftop of his home, she scanned her surroundings and could see the rooftops of different homes far and spread out. Once she was sure there wasn't anyone watching her, she oozed inside the chimney and came out inside the living room of God's house a little dusty. To her surprise, Billie found him inside the kitchen, pouring a glass of what she assumed was Hennessy.

Billie hunched down beside the living room couch and pulled out two throwing knives, which gleamed from the lights hanging on the Christmas tree. Hearing God put up the bottle of alcohol, she took a deep breath and sprung from behind the couch. Her gloved hand swung out and unleashed the throwing knives, which spun around like small helicopter propellers, whizzing through the air. The first knife exploded the glass and splashed Hennessy all over God's shirt. The second knife struck him in his arm. He made a painful groan and looked to his arm. Seeing it bleeding with the knife lodged in it, God pulled out the knife and saw that it was dripping blood.

"Fuuuck!" God said and dropped the knife. He looked up and saw someone dressed in all black and wearing a ski mask over their face. The assailant leaped up in the air and kicked him in the chest, sending him rocketing against the refrigerator. The alphabet magnets on the refrigerator fell to the kitchen floor from the impact of God's body. God slid down to the floor, looking up at his assailant. He could have sworn he saw tears coming from his eyes.

"I'm sorry, but I've gotta do this," Billie spoke from behind the ski mask and launched more of the throwing knives at him. They gleamed as they spun through the air, stabbing into God's torso. He threw his head back and hollered out in pain. Seeing his attacker pull out two more of the throwing knives as he approached him, the Glock that he kept stashed inside of the kitchen drawer came to his mind. He sprung to his feet as fast as he could and yanked the drawer out, emptying out all of its contents. The black gun fell to the floor. He went to pick it up, and two of the throwing knives lodged halfway into his hand, dotting his shirt up with blood. He howled in pain and fell back against the kitchen counter, falling back against the floor. Lying where he was, God stared up at the ceiling. He found his vision getting blurry, and his breaths growing shorter.

"Finish it—finish it—" God gasped, trying to catch his breath, seeing his assailant standing over him with one more throwing knife. He was sure that *this* knife was going to be the one to take his life. God stared up into the holes of the attacker's ski mask, meeting his eyes. He was sure that the assailant's eyes were dripping tears now, because they poured down in torrents from the brims of his eyes, splashing on his face and shirt. God's face balled up. He didn't understand why the nigga that was trying to kill him was crying. Then, recognition went off inside of his head, and it dawned on him who it was that was about to finish him off. "Billie? But—but—but why, baby? I thought—I thought chu loved me."

Right then, Billie pulled the ski mask from off her face and held it down at her side. She was crying like a new born baby, teardrops splashing on the kitchen floor against the blood that God had dropped. "I do love you, God, I do." She broke down crying and dropped the throwing knife, covering the lower half of her face. She bawled loud and hard, hating herself for what she was about to do. She rushed over to him and cradled him in her arms, still crying. "I'm sorry. I'm so sorry. I'm not gonna do it. I can't do it. I love you, God. I love you so much." Billie kissed him on his forehead and then on his lips. She plucked all of the throwing knives from out of his wounds and tossed them on the floor. She then dipped off down the hallway, locking Charity's door so she wouldn't come out and see what she'd done to her father. Afterwards, she went inside of God's bedroom and snatched the pillowcases from off of the pillows. She ran back inside of the kitchen and tied the pillowcases around the areas of God's body to ease his bleeding. "I'm going to call the police so they can come with an ambulance, okay? Just hold on. Stay with me."

God watched as Billie grabbed his house phone. She was about to dial 9-1-1, until God spoke to her again. "Don't, don't call 'em yet. I wanna know why. I wanna know why you tried to kill me."

Billie walked over to him and kneeled down. She went on to tell him about her reason for trying to kill him. She then went on to confess that she really did love him, and that was the reason that she couldn't go through with killing him. She asked if he could ever forgive her, but he didn't answer. Instead, he turned away from her, shut his eyelids and tears shot down his face. This hurt Billie's heart because she knew that she'd lost him forever. Still, she was going to call the police so he could get the help he needed.

Billie called the police and disconnected the call. She then pulled the ski mask back over her face, kissed God goodbye, and ran out of the house.

# Chapter 8

### *The next day*

Joaquin was inside the laundry room, folding up the undergarments. As he was handling the task at hand, Officer Murtaugh walked near him and started talking to him. Although the corrections officer was talking, his eyes were scanning his surroundings, observing the other inmates that were working inside of the facility.

"Torres, what if I was to tell you I gotta 'notha lick for you?" Murtaugh asked, pretending like he wasn't holding a conversation with Joaquin. He was looking at everything except for him while talking. Small talk had led to the two of them swapping stories about each other's lives. They had ended up growing quite the bond during Joaquin's incarceration, and although they'd never say it out loud, they considered each other friends.

"I'd say show me that man and I'll show you a dead body," Joaquin answered as he continued to fold up the undergarments. Through their conversing, Murtaugh had discovered that Joaquin was a former hitter for a very infamous cartel he refused to name. Upon receiving this knowledge, the corrections officer thought about how he could exploit Joaquin's talents and make them both a profit. If there was one thing about Murtaugh that you could count on, he was always thinking of ways to make a buck.

"Alright, here's the deal, thirty large."

"Okay," Joaquin nodded, liking the amount he'd heard. He'd didn't always do contract killings, so he didn't have a set price. But he'd usually take a job for nothing less than twenty bands, of which fifteen percent went to Murtaugh for his managing fee. "Who's the nigga that's tryna see God?"

"Look alive." Murtaugh nodded across the way to an inmate that was handling the dirty under garments and then walked away. When Joaquin looked up, he saw Raheem, who wasn't paying him any mind. Frog was locked up for being a convicted felon with an unregistered firearm. He was looking at some serious time based on his record, but he'd hired an attorney that swore he could get him out of the mess he was in, considering the police had unlawfully searched his vehicle.

*You're a dead man walking, homeboy,* Joaquin thought as he stared at Raheem, continuing to fold the undergarments. *A dead man walking!*

\*\*\*

### Three days before Christmas

God was finally released from UCLA hospital. His Asian female nurse rolled him out of his room in a wheelchair, and hopped on the elevator. When they got off of the elevator, they found a big brolic nigga standing before them in a hoodie. He was wearing black sunglasses and black jeans. The nurse seemed to be afraid of him until he smiled, revealing a shiny mouth full of gold which spelled out his name: Buck Wild.

"You—you know him?" the nurse asked, with fear in her eyes.

God threw his head back, like, *What's up?* to his goon, Buck Wild. "Yeah, this my man Buck Wild."

"I got it from here, Ms. Kim," Buck Wild called the terrified nurse by the name on her white plastic tag, as he grabbed the handles of God's wheelchair.

"Okay. You have a good one, Mr. Purdy." Nurse Kim waved goodbye to God, watching Buck Wild's back as he rolled him down the hallway. She then ducked inside an elevator that had just arrived and was going back up.

"You doing alright, big dog?" Buck Wild asked God, as he rolled him past people coming and going through the hospital. They moved through civilians and sheriffs.

"I'm straight. A nigga like me built Ford-tough," God replied.

"Right, right, right." Buck Wild nodded, knowing that God was one of the hardest niggaz he'd ever met.

Right then God's cell phone vibrated and rang. He fished it out of his pocket and looked at the screen. Seeing who it was hitting him up, he answered the caller, smiling.

"Heyyyyy, my beautiful baby girl? How are you? Yes, I just got released from the hospital. Yes, all of my boo boos are better. I have a few things I have to take care of and then we're all going out for pancakes at your favorite restaurant. Yep, that's right. IHOP. Okay. I love you, too. Put Momma Jones on the phone. Hey, Momma Jones. Yeah, I'll be there in a couple of hours. I gotta few moves I needa make. Thanks for taking care of my princess. I know, but, still. No matter what chu say, I'ma hit cho hand with something. See, I knew you'd say that." He chuckled. "Okay. Talk to you later." He disconnected the call, and kept the cellular in his hand.

God narrowed his eyelids into slits when he crossed the threshold outside, engaging the beaming sun. He found himself at the curb. Four of his buff-ass goons were surrounding his bullet-proof black on black Suburban truck on chromed-out twenty-four inch rims and tires. They were all wearing either black T-shirts, or black wife beaters, with gold Cuban link chains around their necks. They were also wearing black sunglasses to combat the sun. You could tell by the bulges underneath their shirts that they were packing some serious heat. Every last one of these men had bird wings tattooed on their back, and a GA (God's Angels) on their hand. These were God's Angels.

One of the buff-ass goons opened the back door of God's Suburban, and stood aside, so he could climb inside. Buck Wild helped God to his feet and aided him into getting into the backseat. The buff-ass goon slammed the door shut, while Buck Wild rolled the wheelchair back inside the hospital. He then jumped in behind the wheel of that big ass Suburban and drove off. As he drove out of the hospital parking lot, one of the goons rolled up a fat ass blunt, fired it up and gave it to God.

"Good looking out," God dapped him up and partook in the bleezy, smoke wafting all around him.

"So, boss-man, what chu plan on doing 'bout ol' girl that faded you?" Buck Wild asked, glancing up at the rearview mirror at God, who he saw blowing out more kush smoke.

"You already know my get down, my nigga." God continued to puff on the blunt, filling the confinements of the truck with more smoke. He stared out of the passenger window. "You already know." His face twisted into a scowl. He then made another phone call, continuing to smoke.

\*\*\*

Buck Wild pulled up inside the parking lot of the establishment that they were going to go inside of. He looked up into the rearview mirror as he addressed God, who was now smoking the roach end of his blunt.

"You sure you wanna go through with this, my nigga?" Buck Wild asked God.

"Yeah. I'm sure. I'm not changing my fucking mind, so please don't ask me again." God dabbed out what was left of the blunt and blew out smoke. "Y'all come on. I'ma need y'all help with this shit." One of the goons opened the back door of the Suburban, and God stepped out—one Jordan 13 at a time. A bright light was shining on him and all his angels as they gathered beside the truck. After making sure that all his angels were accounted for, he mobbed forward with them.

\*\*\*

God and his goons pulled up at Billie's apartment complex and hopped out. As they got out and mobbed to the tenement, the people on the sidewalk scattered, getting out of the way. God and the niggaz with him looked like trouble, and from the look on their faces, they could tell that they meant business. God and his goons flooded the hallway of the floor that Billie stayed on. Once they reached her unit's door, God had one of his niggaz pick the lock. As soon as they entered, they combed every square inch of the place to make sure there wasn't anyone inside.

"No one is here, boss," Buck Wild told God.

"It's all good. I'll be waiting for her ass to get home." God said with a scowl, pulling out his .45 automatic. He then sat on the couch, and allowed his goons to go on about their business.

\*\*\*

"Unc, I need you to watch Annabelle for me—I needa make a run," Billie said, grabbing her purse and car keys from off the coffee table. At the time, Annabelle was snuggled under Kershawn, watching the trailer for the live action Lion King movie. He was wearing his reading glasses and reading over the *Los Angeles Times*.

"Where are you going, mommy?" Annabelle got up from beside her uncle.

"That's what I wanna know," Kershawn said, lowering his newspaper and turning around to Billie.

"There's just a few things I needa get from the store. You want anything?" Billie inquired. She was lying like a mothafucka, though. She was running back to her apartment to see what all she could pawn to get Annabelle some Christmas gifts. She knew if she told Kershawn where she was really going, he wouldn't allow her to leave—for fear that she'd be killed. You see, Billie had left her apartment the same night she failed to kill God, taking only the necessities she and Annabelle needed. Kershawn told her that she should never go back, and that he'd hire some cats to move whatever was left in her place for her.

"I'm good," Kershawn assured her.

"What about chu, baby girl?" Billie walked over to her daughter and pinched her cheek.

"Ummm," Annabelle massaged her chin as she thought about what she wanted from the store. "How about some cheese puffs?"

"Cheese puffs, it is." Billie ruffled Annabelle's head and kissed her on the forehead. She then caressed her cheek and smiled at her, heading for the front door.

"Billie," Kershawn called after Billie, causing her to stop and turn around, adjusting the strap of her purse on her shoulder. "You thought about what chu gonna do about that other thing we discussed?"

Billie looked at the floor, then back up at him, nodding. "I guess you're gonna go ahead with it, huh?"

"Yeah."

"That's what I thought."

He focused his attention back on the newspaper and Billie headed out of the door, shutting it behind her.

\*\*\*

Billie pulled up in front of her apartment complex and hopped out. As she headed for the building's entrance, unbeknownst to her, Buck Wild and the rest of the goons were peering out of the tinted windows of the Suburban truck at her, mad-dogging. Billie disappeared through the door of the tenement and caught the elevator up to her floor, stepping off of it. Stopping at her unit's door, she placed her ear to it and listened. When she didn't hear anything on the opposite side, she pulled out her keys and unlocked the door. As soon as she stepped inside, and slammed the door behind her, God appeared from out of the shadows. He smacked his hand over her nose and mouth, backing himself up against the door. Billie dropped her purse and spilled its contents. Her eyes bulged and she looked around frantically, struggling to break free from him.

"Calm down, calm yo mothafucking ass down!" a frowned up God told her, tightening his hold on her. "I'm not gonna hurt chu. You hear me? I'm not gonna hurt chu. I'ma let chu go, so don't try nothing. Okay?" Billie nodded and he released her. As soon as he did, she dove to the floor, tucking and rolling towards the stuff that had spilled from out of her purse. She grabbed her handgun and came back up on a bending knee, aiming her gun at God. Just as she'd drawn her gun, he'd drawn his on her. "I thought we agreed you wouldn't try nothing."

"I lied." Billie mad-dogged him, slowly rising to her feet, but keeping her banga on him.

God took a deep breath and lowered his gun at his side. "Look, I didn't come here to kill you, so you can lower yo strap."

"Notta chance, my nigga. How do I know you're not fulla shit?"

"'Cause I had plenty of time to drop you coming through this door. Besides that, take a look around you."

Billie's forehead creased as she looked around her living room. There was a big ass seven-foot-two tree in the corner. It was sprayed with synthetic snow and decorated in plastic caramel popcorn, doves, flashing colorful lights, and an African American angel at its peak. Gifts upon gifts, varying in different sizes, surrounded the tree.

Billie slowly lowered her gun at her side and approached the tree, awe written across her face. She took a hold of one of the doves, and caressed it with her thumb. It was beautiful to her. Seeing that she'd calmed down, God tucked his gun up and approached her with a smile. He placed his hand on her shoulder and she turned around to face him. His brow creased, seeing the tears in her eyes.

"After what I did to you, you turn around and do all of this for me and Annabelle?" Billie asked in amazement, tears sliding down her cheeks.

"I know your reason behind doing what chu did. And if the shoe was on the other foot, then I would have done the same." God slowly took the gun away from her grasp, letting it drop to the carpeted floor. He then wiped away the tears that treaded down her cheeks. "Besides, you didn't kill me, because you truly love me. I could see it in your eyes." He swept her hair out of her face and behind her ear, staring deep into her eyes. "My niggaz think I'ma fool for going all out like this, considering you tried to take a nigga out. But fuck them. It's you who my heart wants and needs. And I never wanna spend another day without you by my side— forever."

At that moment, God pulled a burgundy velvet box out of his pocket and got down on one knee before Billie, opening it. Once he did, Billie found herself face to face with the most astonishing platinum and diamond engagement ring she'd ever laid her eyes on. "Billie, would you do me the pleasure of spending the rest of your life with me, and making me the happiest man that has ever lived?"

As tears slid down Billie's face, she sniffled and nodded, saying, "Yes."

God smiled up at her and took her hand, sliding the half-a-million-dollar ring on her finger. He then stood, looking at Billie admire her engagement ring. Finally, she looked up at him, pulled him in close and kissed him. They kissed long, hard, deep and lovingly. It was a kiss that dreams were made of.

\*\*\*

### The next day

Frog was so engrossed in his work—separating the dirty undergarments—that he didn't notice the inmates slowly disappearing from out of the laundry room. He was also oblivious of Joaquin, who was hunched over and moving around the laundry room strategically, a white T-shirt twisted thinly and wrapped around both of his fists. Joaquin's face was hidden behind white T-shirts, which he wore over his head and the lower half of his face. There was only enough room for his eyes to peer out of. And he was okay with that because he didn't want anyone to be able to identify him.

Frog tossed the last article of dirty clothing aside. He then frowned up and looked around the laundry room. He couldn't help wondering where the fuck everyone had gone to.

"Where the fuck did niggaz go?" Frog asked no one in particular.

At that moment, Joaquin popped up from behind Frog and looped the T-shirt around his neck. He pulled the shirt around his neck tightly, and pulled him into him, holding him back with all of his strength.

"Gaaaag!" Raheem's eyes bulged, and his mouth stretched wide open, revealing all the teeth inside his mouth. He tried to gouge out Joaquin's eyes, then slipped his hands underneath the shirt he was being strangled with, trying to pull it free from his aching throat. "Gahhhhh!"

"Stop fighting this shit, bitch nigga! Just let it happen!" a gritting Joaquin said into Raheem's ear as he thrashed his legs, knocking over piles of undergarments and socks.

"Gaaaagaagaggagga!" Frog continued to gag and choke. Blood clots formed in his eyes, and veins bulged in his forehead. After a while, his lips began to turn purplish blue, and his movements slowed. Before Joaquin knew it, Frog went limp in his arms. Even still, Joaquin kept on strangling him until he was sure he was lifeless. Joaquin, with sweat stains under his armpits, hoisted Frog up and tossed his bitch ass inside of the big gray laundry bin he'd taken the dirty garments out of. Breathing hard, he looked over inside of the bin at him, mad-dogging him. "Snitch ass nigga!"

Joaquin tossed the shirt he'd used to strangle Frog aside. He then pulled out a throwaway cellular, took pictures of his victim and sent them to someone. Afterwards, he dumped piles and piles of clothes on him, and pushed the bin he was inside of aside. He then pulled off his disguise and walked down the aisle. As he was walking, Murtaugh appeared out of nowhere and he slipped a few hundred dollar bills inside his breast pocket.

\*\*\*

### Christmas night

God and Billie sat on the couch in matching silk black pajamas with their initials sewn on them. They were sipping egg-nog and watching their daughters—Annabelle and Charity—open the last of their Christmas gifts. While all of this was going on, Kershawn was in the kitchen helping Momma Jones cook. The older folks were in a world all of their own.

"Well, while the girls are busy opening up the last of their gifts, how about I let chu open yours?" Billie looked at God.

God's forehead crinkled, wondering what Billie was talking about. Since they'd made their relationship official, he'd chunked her off a nice piece of change and moved her inside of his crib. They'd been under one another since the night they almost blasted on each other back at her apartment, so he didn't know when she had time to go out and cop him a gift.

"You got me something?" God asked, pointing his finger at his chest.

"Yeah, why are you so surprised?" she asked, taking his gift from behind the couch pillow, where she'd hidden it.

"I just don't remember you being gone out from under me long enough to grab me anything, is all."

"Baby, I'ma ex hit-woman, I get in and get out without people ever even knowing I've been there."

"Right. I'll never doubt chu again." He smiled. He then took the gift from her and sat his glass of egg-nog down on the coffee table.

Billie watched him closely as he peeled the paper from off the gift. God found himself holding a frame upside down. When he turned it over it was a framed, positive home pregnancy test. A big smile spread across his lips, and he wrapped his arm around Billie's neck, pulling her close. She held on to his chin as they shut their eyelids, kissing.

***

### One week later

Joaquin snorted cocaine from off his fist, getting as high as the Lord would allow. Ever since he'd joined Blood Brothers Inc., he'd been having nightmares about all of the horrible shit he'd done during his stint with the cartel. Nightmares that haunted him like the ghosts of an old mansion. He found that his only way of coping was, drowning himself in alcohol and cocaine. If it wasn't for his vices and the love of his daughter, he was sure he'd have blown his brains out a long time ago to escape the madness inside of his head.

Hearing someone approaching his cell on the tier, Joaquin hurriedly stashed the small packet of cocaine and licked the residue from off his fist. He wiped his nose as best as he could, trying to get rid of the coke residue in his nostrils. Seeing the shadow of the person approaching, Joaquin lay back in bed and pretended to be reading a Don Diva magazine. His forehead crinkled when the shadow stopped at his cell. He was about to withdraw his shank where he'd hidden it, until the man standing at his cell spoke.

"Torres, on your feet, you've got a visitor," the man the shadow belonged to said. Joaquin, knowing the familiar voice, sat his magazine aside and sat up in bed. Just like he thought, it was corrections officer Murtaugh.

"Gemme a sec, Murtaugh." Joaquin put up the magazine and jumped to his feet, straightening out his uniform. He was about to walk out of his cell, but Murtaugh stopped him, and pointed to his nose. Joaquin's brows furrowed, not knowing what he was talking about. He raced over to his bunk and pulled out the small round mirror, where he'd hidden it. He looked over his reflection and saw the cocaine residue around his nostrils. He also noticed that he was high as fuck. He was in a rush right now, so he couldn't do anything about it just then. After he took the time to clean himself up, Joaquin stashed the mirror and Murtaugh led him down the corridor.

"Man, you're as high as a goddamn kite, Torres," Murtaugh said to him as they headed for the visiting room.

"Yeah, I know, but it ain't shit I can do about it now. Whoever has come to see me knows my circumstances and will have to understand I'm doing what I gotta do to survive this madness. You feel me? If they don't, then mothafuck 'em." Joaquin kept walking and looking straight ahead. He and Murtaugh were trying to make it seem like they weren't talking to one another. You see, no one knew about their ties, and they wanted to keep it that way. Murtaugh would pay Joaquin to do hits for him here and there for other niggaz that were on lock. Murtaugh took a fee for whatever contract he presented him with. The problem with Joaquin was, the dough he was supposed to be using to pay for his attorney— he was using to get high.

"I feel you," Murtaugh told him. "Well, check this out; I gotta 'notha lick for you."

"Good. I needa start stacking up some paypa, so I can take care of my family and shit. I gotta start providing for baby mama and my lil' girl by any means. So who's this fool that's gotta death wish?"

"The guy who contacted me doesn't want him killed—he wants 'em to suffer."

"Fuck this nigga do?"

Murtaugh took a deep breath before going on to tell Joaquin what the man had done. The man, who went by the name, Talib Atkins, was a second grade school teacher. The slimy son of a bitch used his authority over his students to sodomize them. He'd been doing it for years, but his sick acts finally managed to catch up to him, when he sexually assaulted the wrong little boy. The kid he'd assaulted was the son of a state senator, who was willing to pay handsomely for the kind of vengeance he had in mind. He wanted Talib to beaten and infected with AIDS for what he'd done to his son. He figured killing the twisted fuck was way too generous, so he wanted him to suffer. He wanted him to live the rest of his life with that awful disease eating away at his body until he passed away.

"Alright, I'm with it, but I want a hunnit bandz for the hit. Once you take out your fifteen percent, so that will leave me with eighty-five gees." Joaquin then added: "I want chu to holla at the boy Antoine. You tell 'em if he doesn't show up to the court date, then there's fifty grand waiting on the table for 'em."

Joaquin spent so much time high, or trying to get high, that he hadn't thought about just paying Antoine to keep his mouth shut. It wasn't until Murtaugh brought the idea up to him that he actually considered going through with it.

"Cool. I can do that."

"Now, we've only got one problem."

"What's that?"

"How the fuck am I gonna directly infect this nigga with the virus?"

"Shit, poke his ass up. Use an ice pick."

"Yeah, that's a good idea. But where am I gonna get the blood, or feces to stain it with?"

"I've got chu covered. You leave that up to me." Murtaugh opened the door, so Joaquin could finally meet who'd come to visit him.

While Joaquin was on his visit, Murtaugh dipped off to the infirmary. He hollered at one of the young pretty nurses that had a thing for him. She loved tall, white men who wore their hair in a fade, rocked beards and diamond-studded earrings. Adding to Murtaugh's handsomeness were his steel-gray eyes and athletic physique. He reminded her of a taller, thicker Jon. B. You know, the white cat from back in the day that could sing. Anyway, Murtaugh shot his mack and got her number. In the future, he planned to take her out on a date, but right now, getting what he needed to carry out the lick was at the front of his mind.

Murtaugh had little mama smiling and giggling the entire time he was talking to her. About fifteen minutes into the conversation, he got her to agree to get him a syringe that was used to draw blood from one of the AIDS patients. Instead of using a shank stained with the blood of the virus, Joaquin would use the syringe to handle Talib's bitch-ass.

\*\*\*

Joaquin was visited by the acquaintance of a drug lord named Alvaro, whom he'd met when he'd gotten to Los

Angeles. Alvaro was a self-made millionaire with ties to some very powerful people. Joaquin had done a couple of hits for him back in the day when he'd first touched American turf, to get his bands up. They eventually lost touch, but somehow Alvaro had found him and sent one of his men to holler at him. Joaquin was presented with a business proposition upon his release from jail. He was told he'd be paid a king's ransom for his services, which was something he loved to hear. With this new business venture, he'd be leveling up, on the money side of the game. He was going to be able to make sure he and his family was well taken care of.

When Joaquin returned to his cell after his visit, he found a kite on his bed, telling him where he could find the syringe he needed to carry out the hit. Once he'd recovered the syringe from where it had been stashed, he poked his head out of his cell and spotted Murtaugh coming up the tier. They exchanged nods, letting each other know what was about to go down. Joaquin ducked back inside his cell and grabbed his stash of cocaine. The thought of committing another wicked act was going to weigh heavily on his soul, and he wanted something to ease the conflict raging inside of him. Having snorted what he'd had left, he threw his head back. He looked around crazily, blinking his bulging eyes and biting down on his bottom lip. He licked the cocaine residue from off his Don Diva magazine, and then stashed it. Next, he grabbed a prison-made ski mask and tucked it inside his pants. He looked at the syringe he was given for the task, like it was a brick of gold, before tucking it on his waistline.

Joaquin took the time to look himself in the round mirror. His eyes were still bulging, and he was constantly biting down on his bottom lip. His eyes were red webbed and glassy. He didn't just look coked-out of his mind; he looked crazier than a mothafucka. Homie was in beast mode now, and officially ready to get the job done.

\*\*\*

Talib was whistling and mopping the floor in the protective custody unit. P.C was a place where snitches, gang dropouts, rapists, child molesters and some homosexuals were housed. Everyone in general population looked at the cats doing time over there as pieces of shit. They were regarded as the weakest in the jail population. Therefore, they were looked down upon and weren't given the proper respect. Talib was so engrossed in the task he'd been assigned that he neglected to watch his back. He was ignorant of the danger that had come around the corner with intentions of changing his life forever.

Joaquin, who was wearing a prison-made ski mask over his face, crept towards his prey. Moving with the stealth of a ninja, he gripped the syringe in his hand and prepared to strike. He had gotten five feet within Talib, when the unassuming had noticed his shadow closing in on him from behind. His eyes bulged fearfully and his mouth flung open. He dropped the mop and whipped around, moving to throw up his hands to shield his face. It was far too late, as Joaquin was already in motion, launching his attack. He saw himself in Talib's pupils, jabbing the needle end of the syringe into his eye.

"Aaaaaah!" Talib threw his head back, screaming intensely. His wide opened mouth showed all of his teeth and that pink thing shaking at the back of his throat. Talib slapped a hand over his eye and tried to run. He winded up knocking over the yellow mop bucket and spilling its murky, sudsy water. He fell to the floor right after the mop bucket did, and his head ricocheted off of the wet surface. Bleeding from his wounded eye, Talib hollered for help and begged for mercy. Crawling across the slippery floor as fast as he could, he repeatedly looked over his shoulder at his masked assailant. The masked man was slowly moving in on him, like he had all the time in the world to do what he had in mind. "Please, no! No, more! No more! Stopppp!" Talib screamed loud and intensely. He threw up his arm so he could protect his face, leaving the palm of his hand exposed. The masked man moved in on him, stabbing him in his palm with the syringe, and everywhere else he left vulnerable to an attack. In fact, the masked man stabbed him with the needle until it bent. His weapon being mangled didn't stop him from viciously assaulting him, though. He stomped and kicked Talib until he was bloody and barely conscious.

Joaquin looked over his handiwork for a minute, before speed walking down the hallway. His speed walking turned into a full sprint, and he found himself hauling ass down the corridor. Bending the corner at the opposite end, he placed his back against the wall and pulled his ski mask off his face. He wiped the sweat from his face with the ski mask and rolled the syringe up in it. As he walked by a cell, he discretely passed the rolled up ski mask to the inmate inside of it. Afterwards, he fixed his hair, straightened out the wrinkles in his uniform, took a deep breath and casually strolled off. A moment later, he heard the toilet inside of the inmate's cell flushing. This let him know that he'd successfully gotten rid of the ski mask and syringe.

# Chapter 9

### *That night*

Murtaugh pulled his charcoal-gray '76 Ford Mustang Cobra across the street from a public housing complex. He looked out of the pitch-black tinted window, and saw a congregation of thug-ass niggaz. He could hear their laughter, as they drank alcohol and blew clouds of weed smoke. Murtaugh took a deep breath, hoping he didn't encounter any bullshit on his way to Antoine's unit. If he did, he was going to make sure he was well prepared for it.

Murtaugh popped open the glove box and pulled out his black handgun. He checked its magazine to make sure it was fully loaded before smacking it back in, and cocking its slide. He tucked the gun in the front of his jeans, opened the door, and stepped out. As soon as he did, the chit chatter among the thugs ceased. Murtaugh didn't even have to look in their direction to know that they were watching his every move. He honestly didn't give a fuck!

Murtaugh was about to jog across the street, until he saw the bright headlights of an oncoming car. He waited until the vehicle passed before making his way across the street, looking both ways. As he walked across the courtyard, he pulled out a piece of paper with Antoine's name, address, and unit number on it. When he looked back up, he realized he had the rottenest luck in the world; the group of niggaz he saw posted when he'd driven up was in front of Antoine's unit.

Murtaugh stashed the piece of paper inside his jacket and stuck his hands inside his jacket. He made his way towards Antoine's unit, where the thugs were crowding the door. He couldn't help feeling like a lamb walking into a den of lions, but he wasn't about to show those mothafuckaz any fear. Nah, he'd been in situations like this before. And these were the kinds of dudes that could smell fear like dogs.

Murtaugh approached the men posted up outside of Antoine's unit's door expecting them to move out of the way. Instead, they stayed put and continued to indulge in their alcohol beverage and weed. Murtaugh's eyes shifted from left to right, taking everyone in. He noticed that a couple of them held their guns at their side, while others kept their hand near their waistline. A sadistic smirk formed on Murtaugh's thin, pink lips—knowing how this was going to go down. It was like he was Denzel Washington in *The Equalizer,* or some shit!

"Excuse me, gentlemen," Murtaugh said and took a step forward. He couldn't proceed since the men crowding the door hadn't moved.

"If you tryna get through here, you gon' needa pay a toll, homeboy," a dark-skinned brotha wearing long locs and a long sleeve red T-shirt spoke up. He stood six-foot-two, and his muscles bulged through the fabric of his shirt. A blunt dangled from the corner of his mouth.

"Oh, yeah?" Murtaugh asked, scratching his eyebrow with his pinky finger.

"Yeah," a brown-skinned cat said. He was wearing a red camouflage cap and matching shirt. The shirt was opened to show the black wife beater and the icy gold crucifix of Jesus Christ he wore around his neck. He stood upright from tying up his Timberland boots, where he left a .40 ounce of Olde English 800 on the ground. Nigga was probably the only nigga in the hood still drinking forty ounces of beer.

"To get through here, it's gon' run you 'bouta, sayyyy, five-hunnit dollas," a chubby light-skinned nigga rocking a Chicago Bulls' basketball jersey and a red bandana tied around his meaty wrist spoke up. He was holding a Desert Eagle at his side, and clasping a half of a blunt roach pinched between his fingers.

The short big face dude standing beside him in a black T-shirt and red Dickie shorts had his hand underneath his shirt. The elastic band of his Fruit of the Loom boxer briefs were showing, as well as the handle of his gun. As soon as the white man made a move, he was going pull out and start clapping.

"Five-hundred dollars, huh?" Murtaugh looked around at all of the thugs. He couldn't see their faces, thanks to it being so dark outside. The most he could make out was the wisps of smoke coming from the embers of their blunts.

"Yeah, homeboy, five-hunnit dollas—Ante that shit up," the chubby nigga said, motioning with his Desert Eagle.

"Okay." Murtaugh nodded and smirked sadistically. He kicked the .40 ounce bottle of beer into the brown-skinned dude's face. The bottle exploded into broken pieces and suds of beer washed over his face. As soon as he fell back against the pavement, Murtaugh kicked the gun out the hand of the nigga rocking the locs. Swiftly, he pulled out an expandable baton from his jacket's pocket. With the flick of his wrist, he extended the baton to its full length. He swung it with all of his might, knocking the Desert Eagle out of the chubby nigga's hand, as it fired. He then landed a backhand punch in the jaw of the dude wearing the locs, and kicked him in the chest. The impact sent him flying back against the door, sliding down onto the pavement. Murtaugh's pupils shifted to the corners of his eyes. He saw homeboy in the black T-shirt with his gun pointed at him. So he leaned his head backward just as old boy pulled the trigger. The bullet narrowly missed him.

Murtaugh kicked the dude in the black T-shirt in the stomach, causing him to double over. He followed up by whacking him across his face, and sweeping his right leg from underneath him with his baton. When homeboy collided with the pavement, Murtaugh looked to the chubby nigga in the Bulls' jersey. He was rubbing his aching wrist and searching the ground for his Desert Eagle. Once he found it, he was about to pick it up, but Murtaugh's interference stopped him. Murtaugh whacked him behind his kneecap, and he dropped down to one knee. He then rewarded him with a kick in the jaw. The vicious blow whipped him around and dropped him flat on his back.

Murtaugh, sweaty and breathing heavily, looked around at all of the thugs he'd dispatched. They were lying around, moaning in pain, and regretting they'd chosen to fuck with him. Murtaugh wiped the sweat from his dripping brow, shrunk the expandable baton back to its normal size, and stashed it inside his jacket's pocket. He picked up the guns from off the ground and ejected their magazines, releasing the copper bullets from their cylinders. Next, he tossed the guns upon the rooftop of Antoine's tenement. Right after, the front door of Antoine's unit opened and an elderly, heavy-set woman in a bonnet and flower printed house coat appeared. She had black moles on the corner of her eyes, and the back of her neck. She bore a striking resemblance to Queen Latifah, but she looked much older.

"What in the hell is going on out here?" Antoine's grand momma—Mrs. Davis—asked, looking around at all of the thugs lying on their back in front of her unit.

"Good afternoon, ma'am, I'm Joel Murtaugh, but chu can call me Joe." Murtaugh smiled broadly and extended his hand to Mrs. Davis. Frowning, she hesitantly stuck out her meaty hand and shook his.

"Good afternoon, Joe. Are you the police or something?" Mrs. Davis inquired.

"No, ma'am, I'm definitely not the law. I dropped by to have a talk with your grandson, Antoine. Would he by any chance be home?" Murtaugh's head moved from left to right, looking for Antoine. Antoine emerged from the kitchen. His left arm and left leg were in white casts with autographs on them. He moved about with the assistance of one crutch, while eating a big ass bologna sandwich. His forehead creased with lines, as he tried to see what the fuck happened outside. He was in the middle of making his sandwich when he heard the gunshot outside. It wasn't anything he wasn't used to, considering he grew up in a poverty-stricken environment. It was that this time the shot that had been fired was dangerously close to his unit.

"Big Momma, what's going on?" Antoine asked, frowning up. His eyes caught the thugs lying on the ground. He was familiar with all of them. Although he wasn't a part of their gang, he grew up with them, and they kicked it quite frequently.

Murtaugh took in the diamond earrings in Antoine's earlobes, the icy platinum Jesus piece hanging from around his neck, and the black face AP Rolex sparkling around his wrist. Instantly, he knew that this flashy mothafucka was the nigga he was looking for. This was Antoine.

"Antoine, I'm Joe. Joe Murtaugh. I'm an acquaintance of Joaquin Torres."

At the mention of the man who had shot him, a look of fear came across Antoine and his grand momma's face. They got the feeling that Murtaugh was at their doorstep to cause them harm, but that wasn't the case at all. Acknowledging this, Murtaugh grinned and threw up his hands, showing that he didn't pose a threat.

"Easy now, folks, it isn't even that kind of party. I'm just here to discuss a business proposition. Trust me. It will definitely be worth your while." He rubbed his finger and thumb together, referring to money. "If you know what I mean."

"Now, you're talking my language," Antoine's eyes flashed dollar signs, and he smiled with a bulging cheek of food. He looked to his grand momma and said, "Why are you just standing there, grandma? Let the man inside." Antoine motioned for his grand momma to step aside with the hand he held his sandwich in. She stepped aside and cleared a path for Murtaugh to come in. Once he was inside, Antoine used his crutch to close the door, and then he locked it.

Murtaugh stood at the center of the living room, looking around. A look of disgust came across his face, seeing roaches moving around on the walls. One of them had a white sack hanging from the rear of it, so he knew it was pregnant. A couple of them dropped to the brown carpeted floor and disappeared before his eyes. Murtaugh jumped back, startled, when a blur went across his shoe. He looked to his left and found a fat gray mouse squeezing inside a hole below the wall.

"Joe, honey, would you like something to eat?" Mrs. Davis stuck her head out of the kitchen, looking at him.

"No, ma'am, I'm fine, thank you." Murtaugh flashed her a quick grin and lifted his hand, palm showing.

"How about something to drink? We've got fruit punch Minute Maid, Coca Cola, oh, and water."

"Ummm, a glass of water will be fine, ma'am." Murtaugh told her. When he turned back around, he saw Antoine using an XXL magazine to smack the potato chip crumbs from off the seat of the La-Z-Boy reclining chair.

Murtaugh looked to the hallway and found the open door to a bedroom. The light was off, but the glow of the television illuminated a five-year-old boy with an unkempt afro and white briefs. He was hanging partially off the top bunk, with his arm dangling downward. Murtaugh gathered that Antoine occupied the bottom bunk of the children's bed. The pieces of the puzzle were starting to come together for him now. Antoine was one fronting ass nigga. You know the type that put a one hundred dollar bill on top of three hundred dollars in singles to make it look like he had a lot of paper? From the moment Murtaugh stepped through the door, he knew that his jewelry wasn't real and he wore knock-off designer clothes. He was pretty goddamn sure that C-class Mercedes-Benz parked outside was his rental. The Benz key with the Enterprise Rent-A-Car logo key ring attached confirmed that for him.

*Yeah, homeboy, is most def' a counterfeit baller, so this should be an easy one,* Murtaugh thought of the proposition he was about to present to Antoine.

"Yo, Joe, have a seat," Antoine told him from the sofa, pointing to the La-Z-Boy reclining chair. Murtaugh cleared his throat with his fist to his mouth, before proceeding over to the reclining chair. As soon as he sat down, Mrs. Davis emerged from the kitchen with a glass of water, passing it to him. Murtaugh thanked her as he took hold of the glass. He was about to take a sip, until he noticed some shit floating around in the water. When he looked up, he saw water dripping from the kitchen sink's faucet. At that moment, he knew he was holding a glass full of tap water. And that was something he didn't fuck with. As far as he was concerned, grand momma may as well have passed him a glass of that gritty brown water from Flint, Michigan.

Murtaugh sat the glass down on the coffee table. When he looked to the sofa, Mrs. Davis had just sat down next to Antoine.

"So, what did you want to talk to me about homeboy that busted those two caps in my ass?" Antoine asked, as he wiped his mouth after eating his sandwich. His grand momma frowned up and pinched his thigh, causing him to make a pained expression. He looked at his grand momma like she was crazy.

"You know better than to be cussing in front of me, boy. Show some respect." Mrs. Davis chastised him while wagging her finger in his face.

"My bad, grandma, damn!" Antoine rubbed his aching thigh, and his grand momma punched him in the arm, warning him once again about his filthy mouth. "Okay, I got the memo, shoot." He focused his attention back on Murtaugh. "Like I was saying, what chu wanted to talk to me about, regarding ol' boy?"

"Well, as you know, his court date is coming up," Murtaugh began. "I take it you plan on showing up." He looked at him to see if he'd confirm his attending the court hearing.

"You're god d—you're right. You're right. I'm fa sho going. Homeboy tried to take me out. I'm tryna see to it that the judge locks 'em away and throw away the key. You feel me?" Antoine said seriously. He was speaking freely because he felt secure. Murtaugh didn't know it, but he'd secured a steak knife inside the casted arm, before he'd left the kitchen to see who was at the front door. If shit popped off, then he was going to jam that knife right in Murtaugh's fucking eye.

"That's exactly what I thought," Murtaugh said. "Listen, I am prepared to offer you fifty thousand dollars if you drop this whole case and let bygones be bygones. All you have to do is miss that court date, and you'll walk away fifty gees richer." Antoine and Mrs. Davis exchanged surprised glances. Seeing that he had their interest, Murtaugh stood to his feet and lifted up his jacket. Five ten thousand dollar stacks were tucked halfway inside of his jeans. He snatched them out one by one and stacked them on top of each other on top of the coffee table. Antoine tried his best not to look impressed with the money in front of him, but his grand momma couldn't believe the amount of money sitting in front of her. She picked up one of the stacks and examined it, sliding her thumb over the top of it.

"Fifty racks? That's all you're willing to offer me for my silence?" Antoine frowned up angrily. He was acting like fifty grand wasn't shit, but truthfully, that was the most money he'd seen in his entire life. Still, he was going to try his damndest to get more. The way he saw it, if Joaquin had fifty gees as an offer to keep him quiet, then he probably had a lot more where that came from.

"Look, man, let's cut the crap," Murtaugh told him seriously. "Fifty grand is a very generous offer. From the looks of this place, I'm sure you've never seen this kind of loot all at one time." He looked up at Mrs. Davis, and she looked offended. He was trying not to be disrespectful. He was just keeping it real. "I don't mean any disrespect, Mrs. Davis." He focused his attention back on Antoine. "Had I been Joaquin, I would have saved myself thirty-five stacks and dropped five on a hitter to put one in your thinking-cap." He made his hand into the shape of a gun and pointed it at his temple. "But my guy has decided to go at this a different way. A way that guarantees that no one gets hurt and you both can walk away from this thing happily."

"Can you give us a minute to discuss this?" Mrs. Davis asked Murtaugh. He nodded. With permission granted, grand momma nudged Antoine and they went inside the kitchen. Murtaugh busied himself checking his text messages, while they conversed inside the kitchen. Shortly thereafter, Antoine and his grand momma came out of the kitchen. Antoine stood before Murtaugh, leaning his weight to one side on a crutch.

Murtaugh stashed his cell phone inside his jacket and looked up at him. "So, what is it going to be, kid?"

Antoine looked like it was killing him to accept the deal. Truthfully, it was. His mind was set on at least twice that much for him to keep his mouth shut. But his grand momma had talked him out of it. She thought about all of the bills she could get caught up on, the new furniture she could purchase, and the new car she had in mind. She couldn't let him continue his haggling and fuck the money up for her. Although she hated to, she threatened to throw him out on his ass if he didn't take the money.

"You've got yourself a deal." Antoine stuck out his hand for Murtaugh to shake it.

Murtaugh stood upright and shook his hand. When Antoine went to pull his hand back, Murtaugh held fast and looked him in his eyes. He spoke loud enough so that only he could hear him. "The money is yours. But heed my warning, Antoine, if you show up on that court date, I will track you down and execute you, your grandma, and little man in there on the top bunk. You got it?" He clenched his jaw so tight that the muscles in it pulsated.

Antoine wanted to say something slick to save face, but he decided against it. He could tell by the look in Murtaugh's eyes that he wasn't bullshitting when he swore he'd kill his entire family. He believed him wholeheartedly. And he wasn't foolish enough to test his gangsta.

"Yeah, I got it," Antoine answered once he'd swallowed his pride.

Murtaugh smirked and pinched Antoine's cheek like one of those mafia wise guys. "Good boy," he said, patting him on his shoulder, and headed for the front door, waving goodbye to Mrs. Davis.

\*\*\*

*A few days later*

Talib was crying and snot was oozing out of his nose. He'd just gotten news that he'd tested positive for the HIV virus. He had the doctor run the test on him after he was assaulted with the syringe. Now, not only was he doomed to die by the virus, he'd lost his right eye, and had to wear a black patch over it. The loss of his eye he could live with, but living on borrowed time and eventually dying all alone, he couldn't handle that. Hearing the squeaky wheels of the approaching library cart, Talib rushed over to the faucet and splashed water on his face. He took the time to dry his face and plopped back down on his bunk, pretending to read an old letter a family member had sent.

"Say, young blood, you interested in a book?" an old short, pudgy African American man asked. He had a small afro that was as white as snow, and a thick bushy mustache that completely covered his top lip.

"Yeah," Talib sat the letter beside him and rose to his feet, approaching the bars. "You got, uhhh, would you happen to have *Moby Dick* by Herman Melville?" Talib and the old man exchanged glances about something only the two of them knew about. The old man searched through the books on the cart until he found the one Talib asked for.

Taking precautions, he looked up and down the tier, before handing Talib the book and taking the folded fifty dollar bill from him. The old man gave him a nod and pushed his library cart along, asking other inmates whether they would like a book.

Talib sat down on the bed with the book. He admired its simple cover, and slid his fingertips over its texture. He opened the book at the halfway mark and found a prison-made shank. The long, thick sharp piece of metal had shoestrings wrapped around half of it. It was wedged in the square cut out of the pages. Talib removed it and held it up, looking at his reflection in the shiny metal. He pricked the tip of his finger with it, and a bubble of blood formed. After sucking the blood off, he stood to his feet and placed the shank at his heart. He held the deadly weapon to the left side of his chest with both hands. Focusing his attention on the wall before him, he took a few deep breaths to gas himself up. His eyebrows slanted and his nose scrunched up, as he continued to take breaths. Once he'd gathered the courage to do what needed to be done, he charged at the wall screaming loudly.

"Aaaaaa—" Talib collided with the wall fast and hard, slamming the shank through his chest, and into his heart. His eyes nearly jumped out of their sockets, and his mouth flew open. He ricocheted off the wall and slid backwards across the floor, bumping into the bars. He had successfully committed suicide. He was dead!

*** 

*A couple of days later*

Joaquin was surprised when he entered the visitors' room and found God waiting for him. He didn't have a clue as to what he could have wanted, but he was curious to find out. With that thought in mind, he approached the table and sat down in front of God. He wore a serious expression on his face while Joaquin wore a solemn one on his.

"If you're coming here to tell me that something happened to my daughter or her mother—I hope the next thing you tell me is that you bodied the niggaz that did it, and put their heads on pikes," Joaquin said, with a scowl. He didn't play when it came to his family. He'd bring it to anybody who wanted it behind them.

"Lil' mama and Billie are good. As long as I'm alive you don't have to worry about them. I came here for something else altogether."

"Oh, yeah? Well, what's that?"

God took a breath before continuing saying, "I came here to tell you that I've proposed to Billie and we're gonna be getting married soon." God allowed what he said to roll around in Joaquin's head for a while. He could tell by the way he was mad-dogging him that he wasn't feeling him. Still, he had to continue with what he had to say. "I want you to know that I love Billie and Annabelle to death. As long as there is breath in my body, I'm gonna make sure they're well taken care of. So, you don't have to—"

"Stay the fuck away from my family!" Joaquin scowled as he told God. He gave him an evil glare, clenching his jaws and balling his fists.

God frowned up and narrowed his eyelids. He wasn't sure if he'd heard Joaquin correctly, so he was going to ask him to repeat himself. "I'm sorry. Come again."

Joaquin leaned closer, so God could hear him. "I said, stay the fuck away from—" he was cut short, when God slammed his face into the table top and broke his nose. Joaquin's face ricocheted off of the table top, and he fell back onto the floor. Blood squirted out of his nose and drenched the lower half of his face. He blinked his eyelids, trying to see clearly. The assault had him seeing double.

"I don't know who the fuck you think you're talking to, mothafucka, but I'm not the one!" God mad-dogged Joaquin, as he stood over him, jabbing his finger down at him. At this time, the corrections officers inside of the visitors' room were rushing toward God from all angles. Joaquin shook off his daze and scrambled to his feet. He charged at God and lifted him off his feet, slamming him to the floor. God winced upon impacting the floor. Joaquin straddled him and fired on his face three times, bloodying his nose and busting his mouth. Before Joaquin could throw another punch, he was snatched off of God and dragged away.

"Stay the fuck away from my family, or I'll kill you, pendejo! You hear me, puta? I'll fucking kill you!" Joaquin yelled at the top of his lungs, as he struggled to break free from the corrections officers' hold.

"You come at the God then you best not miss, homeboy! You got that? You best not miss!" God yelled as loudly as he could, struggling against the hold of the corrections officers. Blood was trickling from his nose and bottom lip, staining his shirt.

"I won't, mothafucka, I won't! Believe that!" Joaquin yelled louder than before. The intensity of his voice grew smaller and smaller the further he was dragged. Eventually, he and his voice had disappeared through the visitors' room exit.

\*\*\*

After their fight, God was able to bribe the arresting officers into letting him go. Joaquin, however, was thrown into The Hole, where he was to remain for the next thirty days. He sent a kite to Murtaugh, who was able to get him a contraband cell phone. Joaquin had a good memory, so he knew the telephone numbers of everyone he fucked with. The first thing he did was holler at Billie.

"Hello?" Billie answered the call.

"You straight up finna marry that nigga?" Joaquin spat angrily. He had gauze in his nostrils and a splint on his nose, so he sounded like he had a cold.

"Who the fuck is this?"

"Joaquin."

"Why do you sound like that? And where are you calling me from?"

Joaquin filled Billie in on what had popped off between him and God.

"Oh, best believe that fool is gonna get his, though. No one puts their fucking hands on me and lives to tell the tale." He swung on the air hatefully, as he paced the floor of his cell.

"Y'all were fighting inside the goddamn jail? Are you two niggaz crazy? What happened to God?"

"I don't know, man. Fuck that nigga. "Look, I know you're not seriously going through with marrying this fool." Her silence let him know that she was going to marry him. The revelation felt like a punch to his gut. And for the first time ever, he felt some kind of emotional pain. He plopped down on his bunk, feeling defeated. He took his voice down a few octaves and rubbed his hand back against his frizzy cornrows. "Listen, call it off."

"What?" she asked like he'd lost his mind.

"I said, call off the wedding," he told her. "You're not marrying that nigga. You and I are gonna get married and make our thing official. My baby girl deserves to be brought up inna household with both of her *real* parents. I love you and Annabelle. So, I'm the man you should be spending the rest of your life with. You hear me, Billie? Call that ho-ass nigga up and tell 'em you coming home to daddy."

"Joaquin, what're you talking about? You still gotta go to trial. You're looking at—I don't know how much time. There's no telling when you'll be getting out."

"Nah, I hadda business acquaintance of mine drop a bag on ol' boy. He's not gonna come to court, so I'ma be a free man inna minute."

Billie was silent as she thought about what Joaquin had put on the table. A part of her still loved him and wanted to make things work for their daughter. But this wasn't the first time Joaquin had panicked when he saw that she was moving on. He'd pull up where ever she was and give her the same spiel he was giving her right now, and she'd take him back. He'd treat her like a queen for a couple of months, and then his dog-ass would go back to his cheating ways. She'd suffered through it because she truly loved him with all of her heart. This time was different though. She couldn't possibly take him back again. She'd found a man she was madly in love with, and she didn't want to fuck things up. She didn't want to do anything that would jeopardize her chance at happiness and break his heart. There wasn't any way she'd be able to live with herself if she did. With that in mind, Billie made up her mind and told Joaquin what was on her mind.

"I'm sorry, Joaquin," Billie began. Joaquin sighed in disappointment. "But I can't." Her voice cracked emotionally and she sniffled. "I can't go there with you again. I'm finally happy, and I don't want our history mess that up. I've found someone that loves and appreciates me. And I know in order for things between us to work—that—

that I'll have to let what we have—go—permanently." She disconnected the call.

Joaquin sat his contraband cell phone beside him and hunched over, bowing his head. Slowly, his eyes pooled with tears and they came sliding down his face. He hadn't cried since he was twelve-year-old. The cartel had brainwashed him, and all the wicked deeds he'd participated in had left him desensitized. He hadn't felt anything emotionally in years. But the day Billie and his daughter entered his life, things changed. He denied it and tried to fight it, but his efforts were to no avail. He loved his family more than anything—or anyone else—in the world. And knowing that he'd lost them for real this time broke his heart, and hurt him to the core of his soul. Before Joaquin had fallen asleep that night, he swore to get revenge upon his release.

\*\*\*

Billie hung up from talking to Joaquin and watched Charity and Annabelle play with their Bratz dolls. They were so caught up with their toys they didn't notice the tears flooding her cheeks. She got up from the couch and speed walked towards the hallway. Once she was out of the girls' presence, Billie ran into her bedroom and shut the door behind her. After she locked it, she slid down the door and onto the carpet. Her shoulders rocked, and she started crying again. She placed her hands to her face and she wept. In her crying, she was getting Joaquin out of her system, so she could love God the way he deserved to be loved.

\*\*\*

Joaquin strolled out the jail facility dressed in the same shit he was in when he was arrested. He wore a smile across his lips, as he looked up at the beaming sun, listening to the afternoon traffic and the birds chirping. He took a deep breath and then exhaled. A moment later, he saw a black on black Navigator limousine on twenty-eight inch chrome rims and tires. The driver's door opened, and the chauffeur stepped out. He made his way around the enormous SUV and stepped upon the curb, where Joaquin could see him in his entirety. The chauffeur, who also acted as a bodyguard, was a six-foot-two Mexican cat, wearing black sunglasses. He had a monstrous tattooed head and a massive body covered in muscles. The South American man was dressed in a black blazer, black jeans and snakeskin cowboy boots, with silver skulls on the tips of them.

"Are you Mr. Torres?" the bodyguard asked with a smile, revealing a mouth full of silver teeth, which gleamed from the rays of the sun.

"Yeah, but chu can call me Joaquin," Joaquin replied.

"I'm Hugo, Joaquin." Hugo extended his hand, which Joaquin shook. He couldn't help noticing he was wearing a silver skull ring, which matched the skulls on his boots. "My boss, Mr. Alvaro, sent me to pick you up. He gave me orders to take you wherever you'd like to go. He also told me to give you this." He pulled a fat ass envelope out of his blazer and presented it to Joaquin. When Joaquin opened it, he saw it was loaded with blue face one hundred dollar bills. "He wants you to get reacquainted with the outside world for the day. Go shopping, buy yourself some things, and enjoy some festivities. Afterwards, he'd like for you to come out and see 'em, whenever you're ready—no rush."

"Okay, Hugo," Joaquin began sliding the envelope inside of his blazer. "The first thing I needa get my hands on is a gun. A clean one—preferably with a silencer."

"Oh, I can get that for you. No problem."

"Good."

"Where would you like to go first?"

"I'm hungry as a hostage. I'd like some really good Mexican food." Joaquin rubbed his stomach. "I'm talking about some *real* Mexican food. Not that Americanized bullshit that Del Taco and Taco Bell serves either. That shit is god-fucking-awful!"

"I know just the place," Hugo told him. "Shall we leave?" He motioned to the Navigator with his massive hand.

"Yeah, let's get outta here. I stay out here any longer—these gringos may wanna lock me back up." Joaquin glanced back at the facility he'd just exited, as he unbuttoned his blazer and stepped off the curb. Hugo held open the back door for Joaquin. Joaquin was about to get in, until two beautiful Afro-Brazilian women stuck their heads out of the door. They were dressed in skimpy bikinis that showed off their voluptuous bodies. The women smiled sexily at Joaquin, and flicked their tongues against each other's. They then sucked each other's tongues and kissed sensually.

Joaquin's forehead wrinkled. He looked from the enticing women to Hugo, wondering what the big idea was. "What's this?" he asked of the women that were obviously meant for him.

"This," Hugo smiled and motioned to the Brazilian beauties, "is your festivities." He produced a row of six gold foil-wrapped lubricated condoms, and passed them to Joaquin. Joaquin smiled, took the condoms, and slid into the back seat of the stretch Navigator. Once he slammed the door behind him, Hugo walked around to the driver's side and hopped in. He cranked up the enormous SUV and pulled into traffic, driving off.

***

### That night

God, Billie and the girls sat on the couch, under a blanket, eating popcorn and laughing at Frozen 2. The doorbell chimed and stole God and Billie's attention. They looked at the door, then back at each other.

"Pizza," God and Billie said in unison.

"Mommy, we're all outta popcorn," Annabelle told her mother, and flashed the big empty bowl, with popcorn residue in it.

Billie took the bowl and looked to God. "I'll get the popcorn while you get the pizza, deal?" She extended her fist toward him.

"Deal," God agreed and dapped her up. They then kissed, threw the blankets off them and went their separate ways. Billie went to the kitchen and God went to the front door.

The doorbell chimed once again.

"I'm coming, I'm coming!" God said, as he approached the door, pulling a knot of one hundred dollar bills from out of his pocket.

"Bae!" Billie called out to God from inside of the kitchen.

"What's up?" God asked, preparing to move the chain from the front door.

"Don't forget the Pepsi."

"Okay," he responded, removing the chain from the door and unlocking it. He twisted the knob and pulled open the door. His eyes doubled in size, and his mouth hung open, when he saw Joaquin standing on the other side.

Joaquin smiled at him wickedly while holding his right hand behind his back. Suddenly, his eyebrows arched, his nose scrunched up, and a vein on his temple bulged. He brought his right hand up and pointed a SIG Sauer P226 with a silencer in God's face.

"I told you to stay the fuck away from my family, or I'd kill you, didn't I?"

*To Be Continued...*
The Realest Killaz 2
Coming Soon

# Submission Guideline

Submit the first three chapters of your completed manuscript to ldpsubmissions@gmail.com, subject line: Your book's title. The manuscript must be in a .doc file and sent as an attachment. Document should be in Times New Roman, double spaced and in size 12 font. Also, provide your synopsis and full contact information. If sending multiple submissions, they must each be in a separate email.

Have a story but no way to send it electronically? You can still submit to LDP/Ca$h Presents. Send in the first three chapters, written or typed, of your completed manuscript to:

**LDP: Submissions Dept**
**Po Box 944**
**Stockbridge, Ga 30281**

*DO NOT send original manuscript. Must be a duplicate.*

Provide your synopsis and a cover letter containing your full contact information.

Thanks for considering LDP and Ca$h Presents.

**Coming Soon from Lock Down Publications/Ca$h Presents**

BOW DOWN TO MY GANGSTA

By **Ca$h**

TORN BETWEEN TWO

By **Coffee**

THE STREETS STAINED MY SOUL **II**

By **Marcellus Allen**

BLOOD OF A BOSS **VI**

SHADOWS OF THE GAME II

By **Askari**

LOYAL TO THE GAME **IV**

By **T.J. & Jelissa**

A DOPEBOY'S PRAYER **II**

By **Eddie "Wolf" Lee**

IF LOVING YOU IS WRONG... **III**

By **Jelissa**

TRUE SAVAGE **VII**

MIDNIGHT CARTEL III

DOPE BOY MAGIC IV

CITY OF KINGZ II

By **Chris Green**

BLAST FOR ME **III**

A SAVAGE DOPEBOY III

CUTTHROAT MAFIA II

By **Ghost**

A HUSTLER'S DECEIT III

KILL ZONE **II**

BAE BELONGS TO ME III

A DOPE BOY'S QUEEN II

By **Aryanna**

COKE KINGS V

KING OF THE TRAP II

By **T.J. Edwards**

GORILLAZ IN THE BAY V

**De'Kari**

THE STREETS ARE CALLING II

**Duquie Wilson**

KINGPIN KILLAZ IV

STREET KINGS III

PAID IN BLOOD III

CARTEL KILLAZ IV

DOPE GODS II

**Hood Rich**

SINS OF A HUSTLA II

**ASAD**

KINGZ OF THE GAME V

**Playa Ray**

SLAUGHTER GANG IV

RUTHLESS HEART IV

By **Willie Slaughter**

THE HEART OF A SAVAGE III

By **Jibril Williams**

FUK SHYT II

**By Blakk Diamond**

FEAR MY GANGSTA 5

THE REALEST KILLAZ II

**By Tranay Adams**

TRAP GOD II

**By Troublesome**

YAYO IV

A SHOOTER'S AMBITION III

**By S. Allen**

GHOST MOB

**Stilloan Robinson**

KINGPIN DREAMS III

**By Paper Boi Rari**

CREAM

**By Yolanda Moore**

SON OF A DOPE FIEND II

**By Renta**

FOREVER GANGSTA II

GLOCKS ON SATIN SHEETS III

**By Adrian Dulan**

LOYALTY AIN'T PROMISED II

**By Keith Williams**

THE PRICE YOU PAY FOR LOVE II

DOPE GIRL MAGIC III

**By Destiny Skai**

CONFESSIONS OF A GANGSTA II

**By Nicholas Lock**

I'M NOTHING WITHOUT HIS LOVE II

**By Monet Dragun**

CAUGHT UP IN THE LIFE III

**By Robert Baptiste**

LIFE OF A SAVAGE IV

A GANGSTA'S QUR'AN II

By **Romell Tukes**

QUIET MONEY III

THUG LIFE II

By **Trai'Quan**

THE STREETS MADE ME III

By **Larry D. Wright**

THE ULTIMATE SACRIFICE VI

IF YOU CROSS ME ONCE II

ANGEL III

By **Anthony Fields**

THE LIFE OF A HOOD STAR

**By Ca$h & Rashia Wilson**


## Available Now


RESTRAINING ORDER **I & II**

By **CA$H & Coffee**

LOVE KNOWS NO BOUNDARIES **I II & III**

By **Coffee**

RAISED AS A GOON I, II, III & IV

BRED BY THE SLUMS I, II, III

BLAST FOR ME I & II

ROTTEN TO THE CORE I II III

A BRONX TALE I, II, III

DUFFEL BAG CARTEL I II III IV

HEARTLESS GOON I II III IV

A SAVAGE DOPEBOY I II

HEARTLESS GOON I II III

DRUG LORDS I II III

CUTTHROAT MAFIA

By **Ghost**

LAY IT DOWN **I & II**

LAST OF A DYING BREED

BLOOD STAINS OF A SHOTTA I & II III

By **Jamaica**

LOYAL TO THE GAME I II III

LIFE OF SIN I, II III

By **TJ & Jelissa**

BLOODY COMMAS I & II

SKI MASK CARTEL I  II & III

KING OF NEW YORK I II,III IV V

RISE TO POWER I II III

COKE KINGS I II III IV

BORN HEARTLESS I II III IV

KING OF THE TRAP

By **T.J. Edwards**

IF LOVING HIM IS WRONG…I & II

LOVE ME EVEN WHEN IT HURTS I II III

By **Jelissa**

WHEN THE STREETS CLAP BACK I & II III

THE HEART OF A SAVAGE I II

By **Jibril Williams**

A DISTINGUISHED THUG STOLE MY HEART I II & III

LOVE SHOULDN'T HURT I II III IV

RENEGADE BOYS I II III IV

PAID IN KARMA I II III

By **Meesha**

A GANGSTER'S CODE I &, II III

A GANGSTER'S SYN I II III

THE SAVAGE LIFE I II III

CHAINED TO THE STREETS I II III

By **J-Blunt**

PUSH IT TO THE LIMIT

By **Bre' Hayes**

BLOOD OF A BOSS **I, II, III, IV, V**

SHADOWS OF THE GAME

By **Askari**

THE STREETS BLEED MURDER **I, II & III**

THE HEART OF A GANGSTA I II& III

By **Jerry Jackson**

CUM FOR ME I II III IV V

An **LDP Erotica Collaboration**

BRIDE OF A HUSTLA **I  II & II**

THE FETTI GIRLS **I, II& III**

CORRUPTED BY A GANGSTA I, II III, IV

BLINDED BY HIS LOVE

THE PRICE YOU PAY FOR LOVE

DOPE GIRL MAGIC I II

By **Destiny Skai**

WHEN A GOOD GIRL GOES BAD

By **Adrienne**

THE COST OF LOYALTY I II III

**By Kweli**

A GANGSTER'S REVENGE **I II III & IV**

THE BOSS MAN'S DAUGHTERS I II III IV V

A SAVAGE LOVE  **I & II**

BAE BELONGS TO ME I II

A HUSTLER'S DECEIT I, II, III

WHAT BAD BITCHES DO I, II, III

SOUL OF A MONSTER I II III

KILL ZONE

A DOPE BOY'S QUEEN

By **Aryanna**

A KINGPIN'S AMBITON

A KINGPIN'S AMBITION **II**

I MURDER FOR THE DOUGH

By **Ambitious**

TRUE SAVAGE I II III IV V VI

DOPE BOY MAGIC I, II, III

209

MIDNIGHT CARTEL I II

CITY OF KINGZ

By **Chris Green**

A DOPEBOY'S PRAYER

By **Eddie "Wolf" Lee**

THE KING CARTEL **I, II & III**

By **Frank Gresham**

THESE NIGGAS AIN'T LOYAL **I, II & III**

By **Nikki Tee**

GANGSTA SHYT **I II &III**

By **CATO**

THE ULTIMATE BETRAYAL

By **Phoenix**

BOSS'N UP **I , II & III**

By **Royal Nicole**

I LOVE YOU TO DEATH

**By Destiny J**

I RIDE FOR MY HITTA

I STILL RIDE FOR MY HITTA

By **Misty Holt**

LOVE & CHASIN' PAPER

By **Qay Crockett**

TO DIE IN VAIN

SINS OF A HUSTLA

By **ASAD**

BROOKLYN HUSTLAZ

By **Boogsy Morina**

# The Realest Killaz

BROOKLYN ON LOCK I & II

By **Sonovia**

GANGSTA CITY

By **Teddy Duke**

A DRUG KING AND HIS DIAMOND I & II III

A DOPEMAN'S RICHES

HER MAN, MINE'S TOO I, II

CASH MONEY HO'S

**By Nicole Goosby**

TRAPHOUSE KING **I II & III**

KINGPIN KILLAZ I II III

STREET KINGS I II

PAID IN BLOOD **I II**

CARTEL KILLAZ I II III

DOPE GODS

By **Hood Rich**

LIPSTICK KILLAH **I, II, III**

CRIME OF PASSION I II & III

By **Mimi**

STEADY MOBBN' **I, II, III**

THE STREETS STAINED MY SOUL

By **Marcellus Allen**

WHO SHOT YA **I, II, III**

SON OF A DOPE FIEND

**Renta**

GORILLAZ IN THE BAY **I II III IV**

TEARS OF A GANGSTA I II

**DE'KARI**

TRIGGADALE I II III

**Elijah R. Freeman**

GOD BLESS THE TRAPPERS I, II, III

THESE SCANDALOUS STREETS I, II, III

FEAR MY GANGSTA I, II, III IV

THESE STREETS DON'T LOVE NOBODY I, II

BURY ME A G I, II, III, IV, V

A GANGSTA'S EMPIRE I, II, III, IV

THE DOPEMAN'S BODYGAURD I II

THE REALEST KILLAZ

**Tranay Adams**

THE STREETS ARE CALLING

**Duquie Wilson**

MARRIED TO A BOSS... I II III

**By Destiny Skai & Chris Green**

KINGZ OF THE GAME I II III IV

**Playa Ray**

SLAUGHTER GANG I II III

RUTHLESS HEART I II III

**By Willie Slaughter**

FUK SHYT

**By Blakk Diamond**

DON'T F#CK WITH MY HEART I II

**By Linnea**

ADDICTED TO THE DRAMA I II III

**By Jamila**

YAYO I II III

A SHOOTER'S AMBITION I II

**By S. Allen**

TRAP GOD

**By Troublesome**

FOREVER GANGSTA

GLOCKS ON SATIN SHEETS I II

**By Adrian Dulan**

TOE TAGZ I II III

**By Ah'Million**

KINGPIN DREAMS  I II

**By Paper Boi Rari**

CONFESSIONS OF A GANGSTA

**By Nicholas Lock**

I'M NOTHING WITHOUT HIS LOVE

**By Monet Dragun**

CAUGHT UP IN THE LIFE I II

**By Robert Baptiste**

NEW TO THE GAME I II III

By **Malik D. Rice**

LIFE OF A SAVAGE  I II III

A GANGSTA'S QUR'AN

**By Romell Tukes**

LOYALTY AIN'T PROMISED

**By Keith Williams**

QUIET MONEY I II

THUG LIFE

Tranay Adams

By **Trai'Quan**
THE STREETS MADE ME I II
By **Larry D. Wright**
THE ULTIMATE SACRIFICE I, II, III, IV, V
KHADIFI
IF YOU CROSS ME ONCE
ANGEL I II
By **Anthony Fields**
THE LIFE OF A HOOD STAR
By **Ca$h & Rashia Wilson**

**BOOKS BY LDP'S CEO, CA$H**

TRUST IN NO MAN

TRUST IN NO MAN 2

TRUST IN NO MAN 3

BONDED BY BLOOD

SHORTY GOT A THUG

THUGS CRY

THUGS CRY 2

THUGS CRY 3

TRUST NO BITCH

TRUST NO BITCH 2

TRUST NO BITCH 3

TIL MY CASKET DROPS

RESTRAINING ORDER

RESTRAINING ORDER 2

IN LOVE WITH A CONVICT

LIFE OF A HOOD STAR

**Coming Soon**

BONDED BY BLOOD 2

BOW DOWN TO MY GANGSTA

CPSIA information can be obtained
at www.ICGtesting.com
Printed in the USA
LVHW010417260821
696090LV00020B/1770